PRIVATE SESSIONS

Joseph C. Reyes

Created by
Joseph C. Reyes
Peter Frelik

Edited by
Kai Furbeck

Special Shout Out, to the freelancers @Fiverr

Private Sessions
ISBN 978-0-9990379-0-4

First Edition

Contact the author:
JoeReyes.NYC
twitter.com/joethetrainer
IMDB.me/josephcreyes

To My Loving Family.

Table of Contents

Preface 9

Introduction..11

The Grand ol' Halloween Party....................................13

The Grand Tour..23

The Matriarch..31

Your Enthusiasm is Appreciated 35

Vegans Be Damned..45

Orgies and Cocaine..51

Boys Night Out 59

Happy Ending 73

Try the Crema Segrato..87

Rise and Grind...97

Slag Bitches Took My Room 101

'Roids all the Rage 107

Caught by the Short and Curlies...............................119

It's all Coolio... 127

I'm an Asshole. 129

Pet The Baby... 137

Highly Inappropriate Harvey....................................143

How About Some Head Instead?...............................145

I Was Hoping We Could Hang out Tonight.......... 153

Another Fine Mess..165

You Don't Look So Good..169

Questions...173

Worst Week Ever, Be Like..175

Greenmailin' Like a Boss 179

Epilogue 183

Preface

Set in current day New York City. *Private Sessions* is a story that delves into the lives of a zealous group of personal trainers that work at The Metropolitan Grand Health Club: The largest, most luxurious gym in the world.

"The Grand," as its affectionately called by its patrons and employees, is the eminent Mega Gym still standing. Barely surviving the economic crisis of 2008, it's part gym, part spa, part country club, and all luxury. Located in trendy SOHO, this 50 million dollar, 100,000 square foot, sweat-Mecca offers everything to inspire heavy breathing.

The members of The Grand are a microcosm of characters that intermingle on a daily basis, creating some interesting and unusual stories. Famous celebrities, sleazy executives, drug addicted moguls, and poor little rich girls rub elbows with wealthy eccentrics, aging swingers, and mid-western transplants, all seeking fortune.

On the surface, the eclectic team of trainers seem moronic, superficial, and immature. But beneath it all, they're people just like us, living with the repercussions of the second worst economic recession this country has ever seen, a time when millions of people lost their homes, their jobs, and their dignity.

Nevertheless, they get up early, work late. They train hard, play harder, and hustle for money. Building their businesses, bodies and reputation. They live for the nightlife, while aspiring for the status, of their wealthy clientele. All while trying to keep The Grand, from being taken over by Fit Corp. A multi-million dollar gym conglomerate, determined to undermine The Grand's ability to prosper.

Issues like mental illness and personality disorders also arise due to the erratic and absurd behavior of some of the characters. Prescription pill abuse and the trafficking of illegal performance-enhancing drugs are also discussed. The trainers in these stories may seem like silly hapless fools, but these issues are serious and prevalent throughout fitness communities in America.

Introduction

I can't believe. You're really making me do this shit! Lol
Jason chuckled as he read Matt's text message.

*Get your panties out of your ass and man the fuck up, my little savage.
There's no turning back now, see you at the party :)* Jason replied.

He hit send, put his phone back in his pocket, and stopped at a red light. He looked up to see exactly where he was—East 77th and 3rd avenue. The light turned green and people began to cross.

While most pedestrians usually mind their business, some couldn't help but gawk and point to Jason as they passed him by.

Jason barely stepped onto the sidewalk on the other side of the street. When a short, overweight man, followed by his short, overweight family approached him. The man wore a small trucker's hat that had *America The Beautiful* embroidered on it. The entire family wore matching blue Indianapolis 500 windbreakers. They all crowded around Jason, stopping him in the middle of the sidewalk.

"Excuse me sir, we're from out of town. Would you mind taking a picture with me and my family? My wife and kids think you look really cool and authentic-like."

"Sure, I don't mind..." said Jason, feigning a smile. "Anything for out-of-towners."

"Great!" said the man as he pulled out a phone and selfie-stick from his overstuffed fanny-pack.

"Okay everybody, squeeze in there together, let's try and get this in one shot this time!" He said, directing his family into position.

Everyone began squeezing around Jason, jostling him from side to side. It took everything in him to remain polite as everyone crammed together.

"Let me guess, you guys from Indiana?" Asked Jason.

"Nope. Missouri," the man's son replied.

Oh boy... Jason thought.

The tourist angled the camera and waited for it to come into focus.

"Okay Bunny, stand in here. Junior you get in closer to your sister. That's it."

The family pointed to Jason and grinned at the camera. Jason, on the other hand, glanced around, waiting for the family to hurry along and get the picture. But before anyone said *cheese!* He spotted two very attractive Asian women dressed in naughty schoolgirl costumes.

Mm… Those are definitely not, standard issue.

"Cheese!" the family chorused as the camera flashed.

"Hey, thanks for doing this," the man said. "We really appreciate it."

"Anytime." Jason waved, walking away.

The family huddled up, excited to see the picture.

"Huh…" The man looked closer at the image. "… That was rude."

Everyone's smiles faded as they each took a closer look at the family picture with Jason ogling the two women walking by.

Oh tourists… Jason thought. Real New Yorkers would get it. They wouldn't have noticed Jason, even if Halloween wasn't around the corner and costume party season wasn't already in full swing. Any self-respecting local, would barely register someone dressed as a Native American Chief as weird.

1

The Grand ol' Halloween Party

It was a cool October evening. The skies had cleared up after a rainy day, making way for the light of the full moon to illuminate the streets below. Beneath the city skyline, traffic lights gleamed up and down the avenues, ferrying slow-moving streams of cars to their destinations. People meandered about on the city sidewalks, circulating like blood cells in the body.

A homeless man pushed a rickety shopping cart, filled with all his belongings. He stopped at the entrance of the Subway Station on 53rd and Lexington Avenue to rummage through the garbage, looking for something to eat. His feet were wrapped in dozens of shredded plastic shopping bags, held together by duct tape, to protect him from the elements. His jacket was tattered and dirty from months of sleeping on the streets. His stomach growled, as he pulled apart the wrapper of a half eaten BLT sandwich. He sniffed it first, to see if it was safe enough to eat.

The Six Train rumbled underneath, pulling into the 53rd St station. Moments later, droves of people, wearing elaborate Halloween costumes, began to emerge from underground. They threw their empty plastic cups into the garbage receptacle, oblivious to the homeless man standing next to it, waiting patiently, hoping that one of them would throw out something good. No one did but one girl accidently dropped a five-dollar bill on the ground while searching for her phone. The vagabond saw the money drop from her purse. He looked around to see if anyone else had noticed. He put down the sandwich and shuffled over to grab the bill off the street. Just as he was about to grab it...

"Ooh money!" Jason said, giddily scooping up the fiver as he made his way down the street. He strutted right past the homeless man, who just stood there in disbelief. *Motherfucker!*

Not too far in the distance, the faint sound, of bass drums permeated the air. Intermittent flashes of light, burst through a window, from a penthouse loft, packed with people; Dressed in wild and outrageous costumes. They danced, drank, and reveled, as if it were their last day on earth.

It was the Grand Metropolitan Health Club's First Employee Appreciation Costume Party, in three years. And as promised, it was already turning out to be, quite the event. Behind the DJ booth, orchestrating a melodic mix of beats was Becky "Bex" Mitchell. She wore a very elaborate, but revealing Spartan warrior-princess costume. Her strong, slender body danced to the music, as she slid the cross-fader switch, right. Blending in another hard-hitting track.

Matt Crosby, one of the Grand's personal trainers, came dressed as a city construction worker. He stumbled into the bathroom, with a scantily clad, little red riding hood. Kissing her sloppily on the lips. He shut the door behind them, pressing his body against hers. Grinding into her pelvis, as he pulled off his yellow hard hat, throwing it onto the floor.

"Damn, I love your lips," he said, pulling away for a second.

"Oh yeah…" replied Melinda, trying to catch her breath.

Melinda moaned softly, as Matt kissed her on the neck. She grabbed him by the utility belt, and began to undo his pants.

"Do you mind, if I get this on video?" Matt asked, pulling out his mobile phone.

She halted, "So you can put this online! I don't think so."

"No, no… I wouldn't do that. This is a moment between you and I. I'm not going to be an asshole, and cheapen this experience, by betraying you. C'mon… I promise… This is strictly for my private spank bank."

Melinda smiled, revealing a set of crooked, coffee-stained teeth.

"Well then… where were we?" She said, putting Matt's penis into her mouth.

His breathing deepened, as Melinda sucked him off. His face contorted, expressing his pleasure. Then winced, when his penis hit the teeth in the back of her mouth. He managed to unlock his phone, open the camera app, and point it down at Melinda. Who was gleefully bobbing up and down; while looking up, smiling at him, with her eyes.

"Ooh... ow... mmm... ow... yeah, oh shit... that's what I'm talkin' abou... ow, ow... aw!"

Matt's body seized up, trembling, as he climaxed, without recording a single frame.

Melinda stood up and grabbed a towel, "Whoops..." She said, like it was no big deal. "That has to be some sort of record."

"What am I, fifteen years old?" said Matt, as he sat in the corner. Embarrassed about what just happened, "Can I get a redo?"

"Sure honey, why not? Some other time though, okay."

Melinda re-applied her lipstick. "I'll see you back at the party, Hun."

She grabbed her things, took one last look at herself in the mirror, and straightened her shirt before walking out and closing the door behind her. Leaving Matt slumped against the wall, in the fetal position.

Back at the party, Matt's co-worker, Tommy Ling, came dressed as a disco-dancing fireman. He moved awkwardly to the music, trying hard not to look too nervous, as he strutted up to the DJ booth.

"Hey Bex!" he shouted, "I was wondering, if you could play that new Natasha Helmsley jam. I hear its real fire, kinda reminds me of you."

But, Bex was so preoccupied, with the set. She didn't notice Tommy standing there.

He leaned in closer, "You should play that new Natasha... " He said louder, trying to get her attention, but to no avail. "We should hang out sometime, after work maybe."

Oblivious to Tommy's presence, Bex continued to spin on the turntables. Feeling flustered, Tommy walked back behind the booth, accidently tripping over a cord, unplugging the speakers, before falling on his face, in front of Bex. The music abruptly stopped, causing everyone in the room to stop what they were doing, and stare at Bex and Tommy.

Bex ripped off her headphones and scowled at Tommy. "Yo...

what the fuck man!"

Mortified, Tommy scrambled for words. "I'm... I'm so sorry. I just... Here let me help you."

"No! Are you kidding me, get the fuck out of here," Bex said, angrily.

"I'm just going to be over here, if you need me for anything." Tommy stammered, as he stumbled out of the DJ booth.

Meanwhile, at the other side of the dance floor, Jason Garcia danced off the elevator.

"Ladies and Gentlemen! Let the party begin." He yelled toward the first group, he saw.

"Yeah!" They cheered back, holding up their glasses.

He casually meandered through the crowd, making his way toward the bar. He shook hands, hugged coworkers, and took selfies, with people in their costumes. After reaching the bar, Jason put down his rubber tomahawk and signaled the bartender.

"Real funny text, asshole." said Matt, stepping up to bar.

"You're welcome," said Jason, "By the way, Bob The Builder® wants his clothes back."

Matt laughed, as he and Jason fist bumped.

"Have you seen Tommy and Facundo yet?" He asked.

Matt smiled. "Yeah they're around here somewhere. Facundo's costume is... well, it's just wrong, even for us. And Tommy... Well, he's just fuckin' up."

"What's wrong with Tommy?"

"You'll see." Matt said. "Say, Jay... are you sure about this?"

"Sure about what?"

Matt looked around the room, concerned, "... Tonight. This performance thing, I mean, what do you think she's going to do?"

"Relax bro, it's gonna be fine, it's a small thing after her speech. It'll be hilarious. We'll get a big laugh, and then it'll be over. What's she gonna do, fire us at the Halloween party!" Jason grinned, handing Matt a shot of Tequila. "To Vanessa!"

"...To Vanessa," said Matt, uncertain.

Just as Jason brought the glass up to his mouth, a hand reached out from behind and snatched it away from him.

"Thanks Big Chief Little Nuts, you shouldn't have." Tommy said, gulping down Jason's drink. "Arg! That was strong. I needed that. Next round is on me."

"It's open bar, dick." said Jason, signaling for the bartender to come back. "And, what the fuck are you wearing! We're supposed to be the Village People®."

"What do you mean?" said Tommy.

"I mean you look like a fucking whale's cock, wrapped in an extra large, yellow condom." Jason snapped.

Matt started cracking up.

"You don't like it?" Tommy asked.

Jason shook his head, "Google much!"

"What do you mean?" Tommy insisted.

"Forget it." said Jason.

He turned to back to the bar, grabbed a shot and gulped it down.

The music scrambled. This time, it was Bex blending in a faster track, without fading out the old one in time. The crowd jeered, frustrating her even more. Tommy waved to her, from across the bar, trying to get her attention.

"Hey... Becky... hey!" Bex looked up at Tommy, who shouted. "Don't worry you're good... you're good"

She responded with a two-handed flip-off, before regaining control of the crowd.

"I don't think she likes me, very much." Tommy said, turning to Matt and Jason.

"Nah." Jason attempted unconvincingly, to reassure him, "She likes you... kind of."

Matt snickered, "You don't have a chance in hell, with that girl." He took a shot and put the glass back down on the bar. "Trust me, that girl don't like dudes... Girls either. In fact, I don't think she likes anybody."

A look of disappointment came over Tommy's face.

While Matt still chuckling, threw his arm around him. "Hey man, don't sweat it. You know that girl Melinda, from housekeeping? She's lit as fuck, supposedly she's giving blowjobs in the bathroom."

Tommy and Jason both turned, to look at her, from across the dance floor. Melinda, obviously drunk, was twerking on a table. They watched her down an entire beer, in one go.

Jason shuddered at the thought, of having sex with her nasty mouth. He turned back to Matt, eyeing him suspiciously. "Supposedly, huh."

Matt looked away, ashamed. Jason shook his head, in disappointment. Tommy however, kept leering at her, entertaining the thought a little too long.

Standing just a few yards from Tommy, Matt, Jason, and their shenanigans was a man, wearing a business suit, holding glass of brandy, he swirled it, as he walked through the crowd. He didn't wear a costume, making him an easy stand out. Gradually, he made his way over to a woman, wearing a tightly fitted, white, sparkly dress, and a white, sparkly mask, to match.

"I believe congratulations are in order," the man said.

"Thank you Thomas, but you didn't have go out of your way, to tell me that here. A simple email would've sufficed," she replied.

"I'm sure it would have; however, that's not the only reason I'm here, as you may already know."

"Of course not, I assumed you came to exploit, the open bar."

Thomas raised his glass, "As much as I appreciate, your dry British wit. I also wanted to see the look on your face, when you find out, what I'm about to tell you…"

Vanessa stood there waiting, for Thomas Richards to continue. "Well…"

"The Board of Directors; Are going to be holding a vote, whether to keep you on as G.M., or terminate you, for gross negligence"

"Well this must be quite ironic, considering, I'm wearing a mask," Vanessa blinked, "But you mustn't be disappointed. We Brits are quite a stoic people, my countrymen and I."

"Stoic indeed and what if I were to tell you, that I'm onto you, Ms. Todd?" He whispered, making sure that it looked like they were flirting, to anyone casually observing.

"I'm sorry, but I don't have the faintest idea, of what you could possibly be talking about." She said, "You have to be more specific."

"I don't know how you managed to become the General Manager, of the greatest gym in the world. Especially, during the biggest economic crisis this country hasn't seen since the Great Depression. But, I'm going to find out and when I do, you'll be exposed." He said, leaning in closer, "I know you're nothing, but a small time hustler from across the pond. Who lied and cheated her way to the top. It's only a matter of time, before I get to the bottom this, and if I find any hint of impropriety, even so much as a decimal point out of place, we will prosecute to the fullest extent of the law. He pulled away. "Now doesn't that *bugger* you... just a little bit?"

"Thomas... I had no idea you felt this strongly," She replied, "I suggest you take any complaints you have about me to the board. Although, I warn you, they will find your accusations, as libelous and unfounded as I do. And, they don't take as kindly, to personal offenses by any employee."

"I know all about the steroid trafficking, the poor revenues in the personal training department and the gay sex in the showers. It's disgusting and deplorable." Thomas snarled.

At that moment, Bex appeared behind them and handed Vanessa a microphone. "It's time for your speech," Bex said.

"Thank you, Rebecca." replied Vanessa. "Mr. Richards, if you are finished congratulating me. I really must get back to *our* party."

"Speaking of *party*, how do you justify having such an extravagant event when the rest of the country, is in such turmoil. Don't you think it's a bit distasteful?"

"You tell me, Mr. Richards. You seem to have everything figured out, or perhaps it's the watered-down brandy, you've been drinking *for free*. That's leaving the bad taste..." Vanessa picked up her glass of champagne, and headed for the stage.

She paused, turned back around. "Cheers! Mr. Richards."

The lights on the dance floor dimmed, leaving a single spotlight shining, brightly over center stage.

"Ladies and Gentlemen, please direct your attention to the stage. Our fearless leader would like to say, a few words." said Bex from offstage.

Vanessa walked onstage with a glass of champagne in one hand

and a microphone in the other. She waited for the crowd to cease cheering before continuing.

"Thank you, thank you for the applause. First, I'd like to thank everyone tonight, for coming out to our first Employee Appreciation Party, in 3 *years*." The crowd erupted, cheering loudly. Vanessa paused for a beat, taking in the applause, like a pro.

"Everyone looks so wonderful tonight: I can't believe how creative some of you are, with your costumes. I'm talking about you Facundo." The crowd turned toward Facundo, who cheered wildly, in his biker costume, complete with assless chaps, and nipple clamps.

"Didn't take it too far at all, huh Facundo?" Vanessa added, sarcastically. "Anyway, it's been a long and arduous journey for all of us at the Grand but with the economy showing signs of recovery and membership sales picking up, we are well on our way to regaining our place as the top health and fitness club in the *world*!" The crowd burst into wild applause. "And, it's because of each and everyone one of you, that this night was made possible. Thank you all for your..."

Matt and Tommy stood next to each other, listening to Vanessa's speech.

"By the way, there's no Fireman in the Village People, dipshit." said Matt.

Tommy turned back to Matt; "I know there's no Fireman, in the Village People. What'd ya think I'm stupid? They ran out of mailman costumes."

Matt, who was just half listening, did a double take. "Wait, what Mailman?"

"Shh! We're trying to hear her speak, you jackasses." Said J.P., dressed as a Greek god, standing a few feet away.

Tommy sheepishly apologized. "Sorry..."

"Better watch your tone J.P., This ain't South Africa. I will tear apart-ied your ass." Matt said, under his breath.

"You have all played an important role in our recent success, and should all be commended for your efforts." Vanessa continued. "Let us all take this moment to reflect on the tough years behind us, and remind ourselves, of how close we came to being bought out by Fit Corp Gyms."

Everyone jeered at the thought of a conglomerate coming and changing things.

"Don't forget about what brought us to where we are today. The hard work, the persistence, the attention to detail, the sacrifices we all had to make, because there was not enough staff. You should all be very proud. With that said, I leave you with this little pearl of wisdom, something I learned in my many years of working here. Never take anything for granted because someday, when things don't go your way—and they inevitably won't—you have to be prepared, you have to be ready to do what it takes to endure."

People in the crowd turned to each other, unsure about where Vanessa was going with this. Nevertheless, they slowly began applauding anyway.

"Because, there is always someone out there that fears your success. They would rather see you fail, than see you get ahead." Vanessa paused and looked down at Mr. Richards, "Anyway, enough of my jabbering. I suppose, everyone should hold up his or her glasses now. Let us toast to the triumphant return of the Grand Metropolitan Health Club! Thank you all, enjoy the party! To the Grand!!"

Vanessa held up her glass. The crowd followed, applauding and drinking. She looked into the audience, watching everyone cheer; everyone except for Thomas Richards. Who caught her eye, as he sipped from his glass.

Suddenly, Jason's voice crackled over the loud speakers. "Ladies and Gentlemen, how about another big round of applause for our fearless leader?" People continued applauding Vanessa's speech.

"Yeah! Are you ready to keep this party going, or what?" Jason continued. "No, no, no, Ladies and Gentlemen, let me hear you one more time… are you ready to keep this party going?"

The lights shot back on strobe-style, lighting up the room. The song Y.M.C.A. by The Village People began to play over the speakers. Behind the curtains Jason, Matt, Tommy, and Facundo came out in their Village People ensemble. Lip-syncing the song to a choreographed dance. Matt pulled Vanessa, who was visibly unamused by the stunt onto the stage, and sat her down. The guys continued to dance awkwardly onstage, spelling the letters with their arms. The crowd loved it. They cheered, laughed hysterically and danced along to the music. While Vanessa and JP held out to the fun the guys took no notice of Vanessa's annoyance, as they continued to dance, twirl, pretending to sing the song and having a great time with the audience. As the song ended, they all slid down onto one knee around Vanessa. Tommy however, disoriented from all the spinning, started to throw up but managed to put his hands over his mouth, while flinging himself offstage before he could spray the audience, tumbling in his own vomit as he rolled into the darkness.

2

The Grand Tour

The next morning, Jennifer Diego stood on the corner across the street from The Grand. She was twenty-seven years old and had just been hired by the gym as Vanessa's new Executive Administrative Assistant. Jennifer checked her phone repeatedly while waiting for the red light to turn. She prepared all night, because she didn't want to be late on her first day. The light turned green and, all at once, a bustling crowd surged into the intersection like a stampede of Wild Water Buffalo. Jennifer's two inch-heels click-clacked on the asphalt as she nervously cut across the street.

She arrived at the Grand about thirty minutes early. Entering through the thick glass doors, she walked across the fancy, Italian marble floor toward Sheila Goodwin, the receptionist on duty. She looked around the lobby in wonder while Sheila looked up her appointment.

"Okay Ms. Diego, here you are. 9:00 am. You're here early," Sheila said, typing on the computer. "You can have a seat, someone will be right with you."

"Thank you." said Jennifer.

She walked over to the waiting area and sat down on a cream-colored leather couch. Her hands felt so good as they moved across the soft leather. Her body seemed to melt into the chair, lifting away all the anxiety that she felt moments before. She stared up at the high ceilings, soaking in the feelings of euphoria coming over her. *A girl can get used to this.*

She opened her purse, pulled out her phone, and started Instagramming photos of the lobby to her friends, using the hashtags #newjobnewlife, #thisgirlisonfiyah, and #aboutthatlife.

Moments later, a tall, statuesque brunette, dressed in a designer suit, walked up to Jennifer, who couldn't help but gawk at her. Jennifer was convinced she had seen this woman in a magazine somewhere, just a few days earlier.

"Hello Ms. Diego, welcome to your first day at The Grand. My name is Melanie. I'm one of the Membership Directors here. My job is to welcome all our new guest and give them a tour." She said, shaking Jennifer's hand. "Have you taken a tour of the facility yet?" Melanie asked, handing Jennifer a manila folder and bottled water.

"Yes… kind of. I took the virtual tour during orientation, but I would love to actually walk through the place, if you don't mind." Jennifer replied.

Melanie smiled. "Great! We can do it now since you're early, ready for the Grand tour?"

Jennifer nodded, gleefully.

As they, began the tour through the club. Melanie explained the various facilities and offerings of the gym, to Jennifer.

"The Grand Metropolitan Health and Fitness Club, is not just a gym. It is considered to be the most luxurious health and fitness complex in the world. An urban country club, worth one hundred and twenty-five million dollars, with every possible amenity, of course you already knew this from your orientation. Feel free to stop me, if you'd rather I… "

"Oh no, please continue, this place is incredible!" Jennifer insisted.

She followed Melanie down the carpeted stairs, through the locker rooms, and out to the Olympic-sized swimming pool. The deck around the pool was adorned with fancy recliners, and looked like the kind of place you'd run into celebrities and movie stars. After circumnavigating the pool area, Melanie and Jennifer got back into the elevator and went up to see the fourth floor studios. Jennifer watched a Vinyasa yoga class, through the glass of one of the yoga studios, as the instructor led everyone from downward-facing dog into warrior II pose.

The instructor motioned to everyone, to breathe through the pose. She then walked over to a woman, who was not quite balanced, and gently repositioned her hips.

"That's Amanda," Melanie commented as they walked past. "She's an amazing instructor. I definitely recommend taking her class."

Melanie started to go over some of the gym's policies, while Jennifer peeked into the cycling studios.

"This is the BiKe FoRzA studio," Melanie said.

"I'm sorry, bike force wha?" Jennifer asked, confused.

"Forza!" She repeated.

"You mean like the Psycle-naut classes?" Jennifer asked.

"Exactly, but Psycle-naut is a registered trademark, which means we would have to pay a licensing fee to use the brand. So instead, we came up with Bike Forza. I think it has a better ring to it, don't you?"

"Yeah definitely," Jennifer replied. "Wow, that's a lot of bikes."

"There're approximately seventy-five Forza Bikes. We just got them in, beautiful aren't they? We spared no expense." Melanie said.

"They look so nice, I love how the silver wheels, accentuate the black frame."

At the far the end of the studio, Facundo was wiping down one of the bikes, quietly singing along, to the salsa ballad playing in his headphones.

"That's Fuck-oon-dos." Melanie said. "He tidies up around here. Ah… Tu eres muy appreciado." She yelled from across the room, in her butchered Spanish.

Facundo didn't look up.

"I don't think he can't hear us," said Jennifer.

Melanie started to repeat herself, "Muchos! Gracias Señor *Fuck…* oh whatever, he can't hear me."

They closed the door behind them, as they walked out of the studio. Facundo paused and looked back, thinking he heard something. Then, continued singing to himself, as he wiped down the bike.

Jennifer and Melanie made their way to the boxing studio where Matt Crosby held a pair of pads, calling out punching combinations while his client hit the pads accordingly.

"That's really impressive," said Jennifer.

"That's Lara Joyner. She's competing in The Golden Gloves this year. She's pretty awesome," said Melanie, walking past them. "And this is our Pilates studio. Whenever I'm in need of some serious postural restoration, this is where I come." She said, taking a proud deep breath. "Let's make our way to the fitness floor, shall we?"

They walked back through the studio lobby, down a grand spiraling staircase. Jennifer was completely taken by the Grand's splendor. Her hands glided down the shiny chrome banisters, her eyes were captivated by the color and beauty of the miniature palm trees, exotic flowers, and lush green plants; That created the ambiance of a fitness Garden of Eden.

They finally arrived on the main fitness floor, where people would come to sweat, burn fat, and build muscle. It occurred to Jennifer, that everyone there was perfectly dressed for the gym, as they lifted weights, bags, balls, and bells. They also sported impeccable casual hairdos.

Jennifer caught herself in the mirror looking a little frumpy. She began to feel self-conscious. *God, I'm going to have to start working out, this sucks.*

"As you can see, all our members take their workouts seriously," Melanie said. "They come in to train with our expert staff, do their cardio, and follow the diet recommendations of our nutritionists."

Melanie looked back at Jennifer to see if she was still paying attention.

"Vanessa vehemently discourages people from wearing ugly grey pants… unless they're trending of course." She added.

"I understand that I get a complimentary private session, with a trainer." Said Jennifer, looking through the folder, Melanie handed her earlier.

"That's correct," said Melanie. "All new employees get a free workout with one of our personal trainers, who are among the elites in the city, even the world. Whatever your goals are, they have a program for you."

Jennifer wondered if any average-looking people were allowed to work at The Grand. Their faces all seemed so beautiful, symmetrical, toned, and surgically reconstructed. *I'm way out of my league.*

Melanie pointed over to where some of the fellas were training their clients. She directed Jennifer's attention to Tommy, who was standing behind one of his clients doing squats, in front of the mirror.

"Bend from the hips, stick out your butt. More, yeah, just like that. How's that feel?" Tommy asked, while spotting his client.

Jennifer watched them for a moment. *That looks intense.* She ventured out onto the fitness floor, a vast open space, with fifty-foot high ceilings, held up by towering marble columns. Sunlight burst the through the giant glass windows, flooding the entire fitness floor, with beautiful natural light. It reminded Jennifer of the rays of light that used to shine through the stained glass windows of her church while growing up.

Melanie walked behind her, giving her space to take it all in. A feeling of euphoria came over Jennifer, as her mind began to shift paradigms. It was all becoming clear, this was the beginning of a new chapter in her life. *This is a spiritual awakening.* She looked back at Melanie, "Oh my God, I'm so excited."

"I know what you mean. I was giddy on my first day too." said Melanie. "I still am. This place really turned my life around. I used to snort cocaine and sleep with tons of men. Now that I work here, I don't feel like snorting coke anymore. Although, it hasn't done anything for the men." Melanie smiled cheekily.

"Wow, okay then." Jennifer said. *That's not T.M.I at all...*

Melanie turned and noticed Bex, over by the kettlebell rack, working a client. "Oh look there's Rebecca. She's our favorite female trainer. She's also a mean dyke."

"Okay?" said Jennifer, pretending Melanie's comment hadn't made her feel awkward and uncomfortable.

Bex was busy demonstrating, a Russian kettlebell swing.

"Don't forget to use the power of your legs, to get the kettlebell up." She explained. "Keep your back in a neutral position, rounding your back, can increase risk of injury.

Her client ogled her crudely, as she bent over showing him the correct form for the exercise. "Oh yeah, I can see what you mean. That's nice, real nice form. I'm not sure if I have it down yet though. Could you please show me again? This time, a little slower."

"Hey dipshit, you better not be staring at my ass. Oh, so help me God!" Bex yelled.

Embarrassed by Bex's behavior, Melanie quickly tried to distract

Jennifer by launching into an explanation of the gym's employee benefits. But, Jennifer's gaze seemed to be elsewhere. Melanie looked around and realized. Jennifer was staring at Jason Garcia. Who was in the middle of telling a story to one of his clients, while he rested between sets of abdominal crunches.

"So I said, Seth! I just got my ass kicked. And he said, 'I don't care. Where are my pills?"

Jason's client burst out laughing so hard. He rolled over, holding his already fatigued stomach muscles.

"Can you believe that guy?" Jason said, handing his client a towel. "Alright, Erik we're done here, good workout today. Don't forget to get some cardio in, before the next time I see you." He gave Erik a fist bump and sent him on his way.

"Hi Jay, how are you?" Melanie said, intercepting Jason.

"Melanie! How have you been? I saw your spread in *Jade* Magazine last week, you looked phenomenal." Jason gave Melanie a light kiss on the cheek.

"Thank you. It was such a fun shoot!" Melanie said, blushing. "This is Jennifer, Vanessa's new Executive Assistant. Today's her first day."

"Ah... Great to hear, welcome to The Grand!" Jason said, shaking Jennifer's hand. "So you're the boss's new right hand, huh? Nice to meet you, my name's Jason. People call me Jay around here. If you need anything, just let me know. I'm one of the old timers." Jason struck a jokingly proud pose. "So where are you from, what do you do, who do you think of when you're alone, with your thoughts?" He asked, kiddingly.

"Well, originally, I'm from Florida but my parents moved to the Bronx when I was young, maybe I was six, no seven..."

Jason glanced subtly over Jen's shoulder, giving Melanie a look: *she doesn't stand a chance*. He discreetly slid his thumb across his throat in a slicing motion. He quickly turned back to face Jen, who just finished answering his question. "...So anyway, that's how I ended up here."

"What do you think of the gym so far?" Jason asked.

"It's still a bit overwhelming."

"It is at first, I remember my first day like it was yesterday. I thought I was going *shart* a food baby."

"Oh! Hmm, it's not quite like that, for me. " Jen said.

"Must be just me then. So what do you think, of your new boss?

"I haven't actually met her yet, but I made it past the all the preliminary phone interviews, met with H.R. twice and completed the four-hour online orientation survey. I pretty much have the job. This is really just a formality. Plus, corporate said they needed the position filled immediately. I've read up on her, I pretty much know everything, there is to know." Jennifer said, naively.

Jason looked at her empathically, as she continued. "I'm qualified and very eager to learn."

He bit his lip, trying to stay positive. "You're gonna do great here, kid." He pulled out his wallet. "Here's my card. Look for me when you're ready to use your comp'd, training session."

Melanie looked at one of the clocks, hanging on the wall and signaled to Jennifer: *time to go.* She didn't want to keep Vanessa waiting. Jason smiled and waved goodbye as the two headed back to the lobby. He chuckled to himself. *She's a goner.*

3

The Matriarch

"Hey listen, if you're free tomorrow night, let's have drinks." said Bill, one of Bex's regular clients.

Bex rolled her eyes. "Bill, I keep telling you, I'm not hanging out with a married man. You're making me not want to train you anymore."

"I just wanted to show you my appreciation," Bill replied, feigning innocence. "You know, to say thank you for helping me get in shape."

"Is your wife going?" Bex asked, incredulous.

Bill fumbled a little, "Well, she's out of town right now, but…"

"You see!" Bex interrupted, before he could get any further. "This is exactly what I'm talking about. Ugh!"

"Look, I owe you Rebecca, I've never felt better in my life, and I look hot. You have changed the way I do everything. Besides, my wife and I are not on good terms."

"You're not on good terms because you keep hitting on other women." Bex said, getting annoyed.

"I see… You think of me as some cheating dog. Who's just looking to get laid, every time his wife is out of town, but you have no idea what I go through. She's not the woman I thought she was. I feel like I've been nothing but a nuisance to her, ever since her business took off.

Bex was not amused by Bill's paltry attempt at getting some sympathy. *This asshole is gonna get it.*

"Alright break's over, get up, let's go! Less talk, more work!" Bex barked.

That's when she drastically ramped up the intensity of the workout, to the point where Bill began to feel nauseous.

Meanwhile, in the general manager's office, Vanessa was on the phone with Melinda the locker room attendant. Berating her over complaints about inappropriate behavior in the locker rooms.

"I want you to put a stop, to this right now! I don't want to hear another complaint, about a used condom in the sauna, or someone shitting in the shower!" She yelled, "Get a handle on it, or I'm going to find someone who will! Am I clear!"

She hung up the phone, breathed in deeply, and folded her perfectly, manicured hands, on her pristine desk. She then, called in Jennifer, who was waiting right outside her door.

"Welcome to The Grand, Miss Diego! Did you enjoy the tour?" She asked, giving Jennifer a quick glance up and down, sizing her up.

"This place is incredible, I feel so honored to be working under such a prominent figure in the American fitness industry." Jennifer said, gushing.

Vanessa looked through Jennifer's files, barely acknowledging her kind words. "Yes... thank you. It says here, you used to work for Vanity Fair."

"Yes, I started there as an intern, those were some great times."

"Then you must know Ruth Thorntonberry."

"Oh yes, I love Ruth! She's such a sweetheart, and great editor. Do you know her too?" Jennifer asked, excited to find common ground with her new boss.

"Sweetheart indeed..." Vanessa said dryly. "Especially, after that hatchet-job interview, she did on me last year," she said under her breath. "What are your intentions with your wardrobe?"

"Ex... Excuse me, my wardrobe?" Jennifer asked, confused.

"Look Miss. Diego, if you're going to work here, you to need know that I expect all 287 of my employees, to be fully committed, loyal ambassadors of the Grand Metropolitan lifestyle. I expect them to exercise regularly, look spectacular, and dress according to our high standards. Right now..." She motioned circularly, at Jennifer's ensemble, "this is not up to par."

Jennifer laughed, thinking she was joking. Vanessa sat there stone-faced, until Jennifer realized that she wasn't kidding "I... I guess I'll go out and purchase a new wardrobe tonight, then."

"Good... " Said Vanessa, "... your compliance is appreciated. Now then head over to the H.R. office and get yourself settled in. I'm going to need you to take some notes and schedule some appointments for me."

Jennifer got up, extended her hand, to thank Vanessa.

Vanessa didn't look up, from her desk. "By the way Miss. Diego, I recommend you review page twelve, chapter 4, paragraph 3, in the employee handbook; where it is specifically stated that "No Grand employee shall post unauthorized pictures and/or video content, about The Grand on any social media websites". Consider this your first and last warning. That will be all, Miss. Diego."

Jennifer stood there, shocked with her hand still out, expecting a handshake, or some form of human acknowledgement. But Vanessa, having already dismissed her, picked up a folder and started looking through its contents. Jennifer put her hand down and walked out of the office, in disbelief.

4

Your Enthusiasm is Appreciated

Bradley Schwartz was a typical Type "A" personality. He believed he was entitled to anything, and thought he knew everything. He'd been married a least three times, to women half his age. He was always on his phone and never in a good mood. Even during his training sessions. Bradley could be heard yelling into his phone from across the gym. Ignoring the No Talking On The Phone, on the fitness floor rule.

Tommy Ling prepared to spot Bradley, who was lying down on the barbell bench press. "Alright here we go. 3… 2… 1…" Tommy counted, as he helped Bradley lift the barbell, off the rack.

Bradley took a deep breath, brought the iron barbell down, and bounced it off his chest. He let out a loud grunt, immediately racked the barbell, and sat up. "What is this? I told you, I want to lift heavy today!"

Tommy replied calmly, "I appreciate your enthusiasm, for wanting to work hard Brad but you have to understand that your body needs to be properly conditioned, before you can start lifting heavier weights. We have to make sure that your technique is sound, your shoulders don't shrug, and…"

"What technique!" Bradley interrupted, "I'm moving the weight up and down. Now put on the forty-five pound plates, and lets do this! "

Nearby, Jason prepared for his next client; writing out the workout, he wanted to add to their program.

Matt approached Jason from behind.

"So my boy that does the club promoting, tells me we're definitely on the V.I.P. list for SauZae tomorrow night."

"Nice… " Jason replied. "Does Tommy know?"

"Yeah he knows, it's gonna be bananas!" Matt said, pulling out his phone, to send a text.

"We're gonna get lit as fuck!" Jason added, "Is Claire okay with you going out? Are you two, getting along yet?"

Matt stopped grinning and got serious for a moment, as he thought about his hometown sweetheart. "Things are rough brah, I can't lie. She's been having these crazy mood swings lately. I don't know. Maybe, it's because she's not landing the dance auditions, she'd been hoping for."

Jason listened to Matt's concerns, taking it all in with a grain of salt. He knew full well, that Matt was no saint, but always the good friend. He stood there anyway, listening to his buddy, without casting judgments.

"She's been going out, with her scrawny-assed dancing friends. To these gay ass modern-dance recitals, sippin' tea 'n' shit. Arguing about where to get the best price for organic kale. Fucking kale, Jay, she's a vegan now." Matt started to get riled up. "She stopped buying meat, eggs, and milk! How is a man supposed to live? When I was a baby, my mama used to shove drumsticks into my mouth, just to shut me up, and I didn't even have teeth yet. Now... I'm burping up wheatgrass... it's been hell man, I'm telling you."

Jason put his hand on Matt's shoulder. "Sorry to hear that bro. Man is meant to eat meat." Jason sighs, "Why don't you try talking to her, tell her how you feel. Maybe, she'll let you buy some steaks for yourself."

Matt considered Jason's advice, thinking about steak. "Yeah maybe I should, but what if she doesn't listen?"

"You know, it's always been my experience. That when you sit down to talk, and really take the time to listen, to each other. Good things happen."

"I guess..."

"Give it shot. Tell her how much you support her becoming a vegan, and that she should consider your feelings too. What do you got to lose?"

"Protein!" Matt quipped.

"Well then, what you really need to think about is what is behind all this. Because, you two are behaving like, cats and dogs. Maybe, what you need to do is be honest with yourselves, instead of blaming each other for everything. Know what I mean?"

"Yeah I guess, thanks man you always have good advice."

"What can I say?" Jason grinned, "It's a talent. Anyway, I gotta go give birth to a ten pound food baby before my client gets here."

"Motherfucker, you always have to take a shit! Thanks anyway brah." Matt said, jokingly.

Jason turned, waved goodbye to Matt, as he walked away. A sultry voice, with a deep Spanish accent, drew his attention away from Matt.

"Hola Yay, como estas?" It was Liliana, Jason's client, exactly on time for her training appointment. *Crap! It's going to have to wait.* Jason thought to himself.

Liliana Dominic Rivera was a beautiful and talented singer, from Colombia. She was in New York, for a few months, to record her first English crossover album. Liliana was curvy, in all the right places, complimented by her long legs and a tiny waist. Her light, brown hair was tied up in a ponytail, her face was in full war paint—possibly done, by her make-up artist. She was clearly either accustomed, or oblivious to the stares she was getting because of her salacious workout attire. She wore a skimpy, aqua-blue sports bra that barely contained her breasts, and yoga pants that left absolutely nothing to the imagination. Matt stood there with his mouth gaping open, watching them walk away.

"Looks like you're gonna have to wait, to deliver that food baby, huh Jay?" Matt said, awkwardly.

Jason and Liliana both looked back at him. "You're having a baby Yay?" asked Liliana, puzzled.

"No, he's just being silly." Jason answered. "Really Matt! In front of a client." He turned to Liliana, shaking his head. "Just ignore him, he's a little special.

"The time was 9:00 am. The morning member rush was over, and the workout floor demographics began to shift. Earlier on, it was mostly professionals who worked all day, and were too busy, or too tired to come at night. However, after 9:00 am, the gym started getting filled with the members, who could afford not to be at work.

Everyone from retirees, who spent more time chit chatting than working out, to the stay at home glamour mommies, who had their full-time nannies take their children to outrageously high-priced baby music classes while they worked out with their trainers, gossiping about each other.

The 8:00 am booty-camp class had just ended. People began streaming out of the studio, throwing their sweaty towels, into the soiled towel bin, then picking up fresh ones as they headed toward the locker rooms.

Nearby, Melinda noticed that the clean towels were about to run out. She called Facundo on the phone, to tell him to bring up a full bin of clean towels, and take the dirty ones back down with him.

Just a few yards away, two older women in their mid-sixties—walked on the treadmill, complaining about the new Sous Chef at Mr. Lings. Their hands never let go of the handles, and they never went faster than, one mile per hour. Another member stood by the dumbbell rack, flexing his arms in the mirror, preparing to pick up some weights. He took three short breaths, lifted the dumbells off the rack, and walked over to the bench. He sat down, lied back, took a deep breath and exhaled forcefully, while pressing eighty pounds into the air.

Bex watched a panting, red-faced Bill run up and down stairs, doing a set of push-ups between flights, barely letting him catch his breath. Tommy was nearby assisting an annoyed but focused Bradley on the bench press, ready to lift the barbell off the rack.

"Okay here we go. 3... 2... 1..." Tommy assisted Bradley, putting the barbell over his chest before taking his hands away.

Bradley lowered the bar half way to his chest, then began to press the iron bar back up wavering unevenly. Tommy goes into help.

"I got it!" Bradley said, bringing the bar back down again for a second attempt. "Argh!"

Tommy tried help again. "No... I got it... RARGH!" Bradley yelled.

Tommy reluctantly backed off. "Are... are you sure?"

Just then Liliana walked by, following Jason over to the squat rack. Tommy locked in on her, leering at her glistening body. He bit his lip as he watched the beads of sweat run down her back, pooling into her sheer tights, leaving a sweaty outline of the crack of her ass. Tommy swallowed a big gulp of saliva; his eyes transfixed, by the graceful motion of her stride; like, a gazelle foraging for food, unaware of lurking predators.

Jason glanced back at Tommy as they walked past, rolling his eyes and shaking his head disapprovingly. Tommy snapped out of his trance, as an elderly woman, came into his line of vision. She sat at the chest fly machine, watching Tommy leer at Liliana. She shot him an icy glare. Tommy shuddered. Suddenly, a look of terror came over the woman's face. Tommy looked down and saw a purple faced Bradley gasping for air. The 135 lb. barbell was stuck, pressing down on his chest. Tommy immediately, lifted the barbell, placing it back on the rack. Bradley coughed, clutching his chest, trying to catch his breath.

"Where the fuck, were you?" Bradley wheezed. "I could've died!"

"I'm, I'm so sorry. I looked away for a split second and… It's totally my fault." Tommy stammered, trying to apologize.

"Ow, fuck… my shoulder. I think I did something to it." Bradley said, grimacing from the pain, barely able to lift his arm.

"Uh, okay. Um… let me get you some ice. Stay right here, okay?" Tommy said.

He rushed back toward the fitness desk, to grab an ice pack, from the first-aid kit; Past Bex, who still had her client Bill, sprinting up and down the stairs. She barked at him, to pick up the pace. This time however, on his way down, Bill's legs gave out, wobbling on each step. Barely able to take another step, he stumbled forward, grabbing the banister, before collapsing from exhaustion. Bill lay there, gasping for air, resting his head on the edge of a step. *My head weighs a hundred pounds*, he thought to himself, as he stared at the ceiling, trying to catch his breath.

Bex stood over him, scowling at him, with contempt. She tossed him, a rolled up towel. It landed on his chest but rolled off before he could grab it. She knelt down, to his level and looked at her stopwatch.

"Looks like times up, for today." She smirked.

"Are you trying to kill me?" He wondered.

"Now why would I go and do that?" She replied.

Bill looked at her for a moment, trying to figure out, if she was serious.

"I'd be out of business if I had reputation for killing my clients. Don't you think?" She teased.

Bill attempted to get up, but had to sit back down. He looked at Bex for a moment, wiping the sweat from his brow.

"I don't suppose, we can do the same time tomorrow?"

Absolutely baffled by his question, Bex stood there in disbelief. She nearly caused this man to go into cardiac arrest in the middle of the gym floor, and now he wanted to do it again tomorrow. *He's insane.*

"Let me check my schedule. I'll get back to you later." She sighed. *What is it with this guy?*

"Excuse me!" Shouted Tommy, almost crashing into her, trying to get back to Bradley. "Here you go Brad, put this on your shoulder."

Bradley snatched the ice pack from his hand, placing it on his shoulder "I'm going to the hospital, to get this looked at."

"That's a good idea. You really shouldn't take chances, with an injury like that."

"Then, I'm going to talk with your manager." He said, getting up.

Bradley stormed off, compressing the ice pack, on his injured shoulder. Leaving Tommy standing there, stunned by what just happened.

Just a few yards away, Jason was finishing up with Liliana. She was tired, unable to do another abdominal crunch.

"Aye, aye, aye mi estomago." Liliana said, falling back to the floor, from fatigue. She lay there huffing, with her hands gripped over her stomach; Waiting for the lactic acid burn to subside.

"You really kicked butt today, good work." Jason said, putting out his fist.

"Gracias, Yay." Liliana said, giving Jason a fist bump.

She wiped the sweat off her face, smearing her mascara on to her cheeks. "But, I still so out of chape."

"What do you mean, you're not out of chape, I mean shape. You've gotten stronger, leaner, and more flexible. You should be real proud, especially with that whole Raccoon thing you've got going on, with your mascara. Wow, take a look." Jason pointed to Liliana's reflection in the mirror.

Liliana turned to the mirror. Her makeup was a mess, she laughed,

"Ju mean, like thees," she said, putting her hands up to her cheeks, pretending they were paws, acting like a raccoon.

"Yeah, something like that, but don't laugh like that. Makes you look like, the Joker." Jason said.

They both laughed, as he helped her off the ground.

"So I'll see you next week? Oh, don't forget, you need to buy more sessions." He said, bringing her to the fitness desk.

"Jus call my assistant. She will buy." Liliana said.

"Sure thing. Let me get your stuff."

He reached down to get Liliana's bag from his drawer.

He pulled it open. Suddenly, his mouth gaped from the shock of finding a giant, vibrating dildo turned up to full blast. It buzzed, twirled and whirled around, all over his drawer. He snatched Liliana's bag, then quickly shut the drawer. Luckily, she didn't see it. Matt however, standing nearby could barely contain his laughter. Jason glared at him, as he walked Liliana out.

"Hey, don't stay up all night at the recording at the studio. It's not good for you." He said, giving her a light kiss on the cheek.

"Aye, talk to my producer, I feel like his slave, but I'll try. Ciao, Yay." She said, kissing him right back.

He waved goodbye to her, smiling, as she got on to the elevator. But, as soon as the elevator doors closed, his smile disappeared.

"Did you do this?" He asked, turning his attention to Matt. Demanding to know who put the rubber phallus in his workspace drawer. Matt simply, burst out laughing.

"You think that was funny!" Jason pulled the dildo, out of the drawer. "You guys need to grow up and stop with this foolishness. What if Liliana would've seen that? Even worse, what if Vanessa would've seen it?"

"Vanessa's tight ass could use a little stimulation." Matt said, trying to catch his breath. "Besides, it wasn't me."

"Then who—"

At that moment, Tommy returned, with a very worried look on his face. "Yo, I think I fucked up Bradley." He said. "I think he might've torn something. I'm so fucked."

"Tom! Do you know anything about this?" Jason asked, putting the vibrator up to Tommy's lips.

"Of course, it was me... I, whatever!" said Tommy, shoving the dildo out of his face.

"What the fuck, were you thinking Tommy? This isn't funny." Jason said.

"Yes it was." Matt interjected.

"Shut up Matt, you're not helping." said Jason.

"You think he'll tell Vanessa? You think she'll fire me? God, I'm so fucking done." Tommy groaned.

Fully aware of Tommy's distress, Jason toned down his voice. "Well it was immature and I didn't appreciate it. It's a good thing. I'm a grown man and can handle such situations. Now let's bring it in, before it gets anymore awkward." Jason pulled Tommy in for a hug. "There, there, my little panda bear. Don't jump to any conclusions. I'm sure Vanessa will understand, once you tell her what happened. It was an accident right? And accidents happen."

"Yeah, like the accident that happened in my pants, when I saw Liliana do squats. Hm... damn!" Matt said, biting his bottom lip. "Yo Jay, you need to put that girl into rotation, because she is too fine."

"Ha ha... Or like the accident you had in bathroom, at the costume party." Jason added.

Matt, stopped laughing, "Wait, what..."

"Yeah, everybody knows." Jason smiled, waving the dildo at him.

"So I'm supposed to tell Vanessa that I let a barbell, fall on my client because I couldn't take my eyes off a girl's ass?" Tommy continued.

"What do you mean, everybody?" Matt interrupted.

"I wouldn't phrase it exactly like that, but yes." Said Jason to Tommy, "And you should probably do it, before Bradley does."

"You mean everybody, like us three everybody, or like the whole gym everybody?" Matt asked.

"Facundo told me." Tommy replied.

"How the fuck! Does Facundo know?" Matt demanded.

"You really think she'll understand?" Tommy asked, looking for some reassurance.

Jason hesitated, for a second. "Yeah, I'm sure of it, plus it's the right thing to do. Then again, she may kick you in the balls, bend you over, and fuck you in the ass, with her massive Satan cock."

Jason held up the dildo like a fencing sword; it was still on, buzzing, and twirling in his hand.

"Not funny." Tommy said.

"Touché pussycat!" Jason said, rushing over to Matt, bending him over the desk, and simulating sex, with the dildo.

Matt squealed, playing along. "Oh, oh my God! Ow it hurts, don't stop!"

Tommy, on the other hand, didn't seem to find it particularly funny. Jason flipped Matt around, flogging him, with the rubber dick. Matt slid down to the floor, pinching his own nipples.

"Hey, hey! Don't break that…" Tommy said, "… It cost me eighty-nine bucks."

5

Vegans Be Damned.

Amanda Downs, the yoga instructor, stepped out of the studio chatting with few of her students. Thanking them, for coming to class and welcoming them, back next week.

From, across the gym floor, Jason spotted her and was immediately enamored. The first thing he noticed was her smile. Her perfect, genuine and warm smile. It was the type of smile that could calm a room. Making everyone feel at ease. His eyes fixated on her every move. His heart began to flutter, even skipping a beat. Ever since he first laid eyes on her months earlier, Jason always went out of his way to be kind to her. He never made lewd remarks or overt sexual innuendos around her, and he never hit on her like all the other women in the gym. No. Jason was always the consummate gentleman around her. Far removed, from the immature man-child, everyone else knew and expected.

He immediately stopped walloping Matt, tossed the dildo over his shoulder and sniffed his breath. The dildo flew through the air. Smacking Facundo, on the side of his head, while he picked up soiled towels. Bouncing, into the laundry bin. Facundo turned around, rubbed his head, wondering what the hell just happened.

Jason popped a mint into his mouth, patted down his hair and nonchalantly strolled over to Amanda. Smiling from ear to ear, hoping to get her attention.

"Hey there, just finished with your class?" Jason asked.

"Yep, the last one of the day." She replied, waving goodbye, to her students.

"What's it been like four months, since you started here and already your classes are packed!"

"I know it's so exciting." Amanda lit up, "I think I'm going to have to, open up another time slot."

"That's badass!" Jason said, immediately feeling stupid for saying it.

"What can I say, I'm a badass yogini." Amanda grinned, cheekily.

"I guess that means you'll be spending more time here, how awesome for you!" Jason tried to hide his elation, to no avail.

"Yeah, I guess it does." She said.

"Hey, since you're done teaching. The guys and I are going to go grab some beers and chicken wings at this charming little bar I know down the street. You should come and hang, for a little while." Jason suggested.

"Aw thanks, but I can't tonight. Steve and I going are to a fund raiser, for his firm tonight."

"Hmm. Steve... Steve... doesn't ring a bell." Said Jason awkwardly, "He's your brother?"

"...Fiancé."

"Ah, Fiancé! That's what I was going to say. That's the guy you were going to duumm..."

"...Marry!"

"Marry! That's right, marry him..." Jason sighed. *Lucky bastard.*

There was an awkward silence, as neither of them knew what to say next.

"So what's a personal *fitness* trainer, doing drinking beer and eating greasy foods anyway?" Amanda asked.

"Oh no it's cool, it's all organic... I think." Jason replied.

Amanda laughed. "Relax, I'm kidding. I can't really eat that stuff anyway. I'm trying this whole vegan thing."

Not you too! Jason thought to himself. "That's cool you know, eating healthy and all, I get it."

Meanwhile, as Jason's futile attempts to flirt with Amanda failed miserably. Jean-Paul stepped off the elevator. He immediately spots Amanda, talking to Jason.

"Oh Mandy. I was right about to text you." He said, as he approached.

"JP! How are you?" Amanda asked.

Jean-Paul was tall, boyishly handsome, with salon styled, dirty blonde hair. His svelte body was long, lean, and muscular. He was a total yoga disciple, with a reputation as one of the best Yoga instructors, in all of New York City. He also had an ego, the size of Manhattan that overshadowed all of his good characteristics.

He leaned in and gave Amanda a kiss, on both cheeks. Jason playfully leaned in for a kiss, as well, but Jean-Paul pulled back and scoffed.

Replying to Mandy, "Truly dreadful darling, I feel like all I do, is deal with imbeciles all day." He said, glaring at Jason, "Just so many idiots, who only want a workout. They don't get it, like we do. Practicing yoga is more a calling, than a fitness trend." He said, putting his hands, on her shoulder.

Jason's eyebrows furrowed. *Really! What a douche.*

"Do you have a moment?" Jean-Paul asked, "I need to speak to you, urgently." He slowly began to lead her away. "Privately, if you don't mind."

"Sure, what is it?" Amanda asked, as they walked away, leaving Jason standing there, awkwardly waiting for her to return.

"First off, I heard your class was fantastic, but you already know that." Jean-Paul said. "Mandy, in the short time you've been here. You have managed to become my brightest, most talented student. I want you to teach my classes, while I'm on hiatus."

Amanda paused for a moment, to take in what Jean-Paul was asking, "Oh wow, I don't know what to say."

"I don't know… thank you perhaps." He said.

"Thank you, thank you so much. I'm honored. But, do you really think, I'm ready?"

"Nonsense… of course you're ready. I've been grooming you, ever since I first laid eyes on you." Jean-Paul said haughtily.

"Okay then, I'll do it!" Amanda grinned.

"Wonderful, we must find time, to go over the details. But then again, I'm going to be so pre-occupied, for the rest of the week. Hm, what are you doing tonight?"

"Well, I've got this event, with my fiancé ton—"

"Darling can it wait?" Jean-Paul interrupted. "I could really use your help. I need to make arrangements for my trip, find boarding for my cat and plan how we're going to make the transition for you to teach my classes. It will have to be seamless, for my students. Tonight, is the only night I have available to sit down and get organized. Will you meet me for dinner later?"

Amanda struggled to find the words, but the only thing that came out of her mouth was, "Um… um… okay?"

"Perfect darling, I'll see you tonight, eight o' clock." Jean-Paul said, "You have no idea, how much you're helping me. The angels will write hymns about you."

Jason continued to stand there, watching them from across the gym, waiting patiently for Amanda to return. But, Jean-Paul kept leading her, further and further away. Until, they turned the corner and disappeared. Standing there alone, it finally dawned on Jason that she wasn't coming back. *Fuck, I'm such an idiot.*

Martha Gladwell, a woman in her eighties, and long time member of the Grand, just so happened to be walking by, witnessing everything.

"He cocked blocked you good, huh?" asked Martha, as she pressed the elevator button, with her cane.

Jason forced himself to crack a smile "Now, now Martha let's not be nosey." He continued under his breath, "You old bat."

"Huh! What did you say?" Martha replied. "That's my bad ear; you'll have to speak up."

The elevator doors opened.

"I said let's not be—you know what, forget it. Here's your elevator, hurry up before it closes." *And crushes you to death.*

"Hee, hee, hee, what a loser!" she laughed as she shuffled her way into the elevator.

Jason snickered quietly to himself, feeling defeated and embarrassed. He decided to head back to work. He turned around to walk back to the reception desk and bumped right into Vanessa.

"Ahh! Sweet Baby Jesus, God all mighty!" Jason said, clutching his chest. "You scared me, half to death."

Vanessa rolled her eyes. "Hello Jason, may I have a word?"

"No really, I think I need to sit down." said Jason, clearing his throat "Whew. Wow! Ha ha. Okay I'm good, but maybe some other time." Jason tried to duck out of the conversation. "I have a client waiting for me and I don't want be late sooo…"

"I'll walk with you then." Vanessa insisted. "I don't suppose you've been watching your numbers lately?"

"Numbers, numbers, numbers. Hm." Jason said, trying to come up with some excuse.

"Don't waste your time playing coy with me Jason, you know exactly what numbers, I'm talking about."

"Coy, coy, coy… Who's being what now?"

"The *number* of people you're training and the amount of *money* you're bringing into this gym have been steadily declining for months now. Why is that?" Vanessa asked, impatiently.

"Well first off, I will answer that question," Jason said evasively, trying to think of a good answer, "but, your posturing is making me uncomfortable. My reflexes are on high alert, so let's get that out of the way, because quite frankly you scare the shit out of me. Even, with those five-inch pumps on. Which by the way, you really know how to rock. You're, like a sexy—"

"Numbers Jay!" Vanessa demanded.

"Well as I was saying, with the economy coming back. The real estate market is gaining traction. But, only the high-end stuff though…" Jason could feel her eyes, searing through his head, as he attempted to explain. "So, with all these new luxury buildings going up, they're all trying to outdo each other, for more residents. These buildings all have these fancy boutique gyms now. With all the amenities, like saunas, hot tubs, and *really* great views. Which, means the older high-rises next door, have to compete to keep their residents and attract new ones. So they too, start putting in fancy gyms, with all the bells and whistles. Now people don't have to pay, for these high-priced gym memberships anymore, especially if they have one downstairs, in their building. Which is awesome for personal trainers because, they go to these buildings, train their clients, make more money, and cut out the middle man, which is you—I meant us." Jason cleared his throat, wishing he hadn't said that.

"Do you train people, in their buildings?" Vanessa asked, suspiciously.

Jason carefully thought about how to answer that question, and not piss off Vanessa even more. "Do I train people, in their buildings? No, no I do all my business here." *She knows I'm lying.*

"*Really?*" She queried.

"Oh yeah, I like to focus all my business in one place, it's easier. Besides, this place would fall apart without me." Jason laughed, trying to inject some levity into the conversation.

"You see right there, there is your problem. You think you run this place." Vanessa stepped toward Jason, looking him right in the eyes. "I don't know what makes you think you have any authority, around here. You don't make any of the hundreds of important decisions that have to be made. You don't have to deal with the people who complain about every bloody little thing, and you certainly don't take this job seriously enough to do so. Yet, somehow, people seem to take you seriously enough, to pay you to babysit them on the gym floor."

"Whoa. I was only kidding." said Jason.

"Kidding, or not Jason. For twelve years, you've been strutting around here, like you own the place. Coming and going, as you bloody well please, never giving a fuck about anyone, but yourself. How long before you realize that you're nothing, but a joke. A tired old cliché?" She said, "A trainer that sleeps, with his clients. Where's the originality in that! Don't you want more out of life?

No, no you don't. This is it for you, isn't it? How pathetic is that? A personal trainer *well* past his prime; Content with a meager existence and meager pay to boot. How cute do you think it's going to look, when you're a middle-aged has-been, carrying around a sweaty towel, for some young surgeon, fresh out of Medical School?

Well here's your wakeup call Jason, if you don't start bringing in more money, and if I don't see more people training. Somebody will be losing their job, starting with you then your meathead friends."

Jason stepped back, hurt. "Hey, hey, hey. Can we do without the insults here? They're more like meathead work associates."

Vanessa scoffed, stormed away, leaving Jason by himself again. He stood there pondering, trying to process the severity of what Vanessa just said. He wondered, what could have happened, to agitate her so much. *I couldn't have done this to her.*

6

Orgies and Cocaine

The year was 2004, the war in Iraq was well underway and President Bush was running for a second term. It was a hot sweltering summer in the city, and a twenty-six year old Vanessa Todd had just arrived from London, the only home she ever knew. The home she could never go back to.

She had gotten lucky landing a small studio apartment, on the Lower East Side. The hermit cat lady that used to live there had died a few days earlier, and Vanessa was the first one to apply for the apartment. The rent was a bit out of her range, but she was determined to stay in Manhattan, so she used up all the money she could scrape up back in England, to put down for a security deposit.

The studio apartment was located on the second floor of a commercial building, right above Doña Cholita's Twenty Four Hour Bodega. Vanessa was excited to have her first apartment in New York City, but she quickly got over it, after she stepped on a giant cockroach with her bare feet. To make matters worse, she had to wake up to the smell of eggs and bacon grease, wafting into her place every morning. It especially bothered her, because she was a sworn vegan. But, the place was hers and she was proud to have it, at least for the time being.

During her first few months in the city, she took on a lot of nanny jobs in order to make rent. The pay was sufficient but she knew she didn't want to babysit children for the rest of her life, so she kept her eyes and ears open for any opportunities that might present themselves.

A year went by in a flash. Vanessa seemed to be holding her own, her name was being referred to more and more people, who needed childcare. Which meant that it also wasn't long, before she had a full schedule and had to start turning down gigs.

One Saturday morning, Carol Hudson, C.E.O. of Hudson Brokers, a high-end real estate company in the city, and single parent of a three-year old boy named Oliver. Had a potential buyer call up last-minute, wanting to see a penthouse in Tribeca. Carol immediately called her new nanny Vanessa in desperation, begging her to come and watch Oliver for a couple of hours, while she was at work. Vanessa, who usually took Saturdays off, declined at first, but reluctantly agreed, after Carol offered to double her hourly rate.

When Vanessa arrived at Carol's condo, she found Oliver crying hysterically, clinging to his Mom's leg, as she got ready to leave.

"Thank you so much for watching Oliver for me, you don't how long I've been trying to sell this place." Carol said, "Oliver, mommy has to go now. Please let go of mommy's leg."

Oliver, holding on for dear life, screamed at the top of his lungs. "Vanessa, please take him, I'm already running behind." Carol said, walking toward the door, dragging little, screaming Oliver across the living room floor. Vanessa tried to help, but Oliver's grip was so tight that Carol had to hold on to the door, so she didn't get pulled back in. Vanessa finally peeled off his little fingers, from her pant leg. Holding him while he tried to dive toward his mother.

"Oh I almost forgot," Carol said, as she stepped out the door. "Oliver has a music class on Saturday mornings, at The Grand Metropolitan Health and Fitness Club. I left the address, on the dining room table. Please don't be late, Toodles!"

"Wait, what class? You never mentioned..." Carol closed the door, behind her.

Vanessa held Oliver up. He was still crying, pointing at the door. "She never said anything about a class." She said, looking at him with contempt.

"No!" Oliver shouted, kicking and screaming.

All of the sudden, he slapped Vanessa across the face, with all of his little might, getting boogers and drool all over her. Slowly, she turned back her head, glaring at the little child. She then dropped him, like a sack of potatoes. Oliver hit the floor, landing feet first on the plush white carpet before falling back, hitting his little head on the ground. Shocked, he gasped for air, trying to catch his breath, so he could let out another ear piercing wail. Vanessa stood over him, desperately trying to figure out what to do. She went into the kitchen, to get a baby bottle. When she returned, she found the front door wide open. Oliver had escaped.

Vanessa gasped, "Bloody 'ell!"

She ran out of the apartment. Oliver was already down the long hall, pressing the elevator button.

"Ollie stop!" Vanessa shouted.

The elevator doors opened. Oliver saw Vanessa, but ignored her demands, and walked into the elevator anyway.

Vanessa darted down the hall, "Ollie no, stop!"

The doors began to close. Suddenly, Vanessa's arm stopped the elevator.

"Where do you bloody, think you're going?" she said, catching her breath.

She grabbed him by the wrist, yanked him out of the elevator, and dragged him down back to the apartment. A neighbor opened her door, to see what all the commotion, was all about.

"Oh my goodness, Oliver is really having a hard time today. Is everything alright?" asked the resident.

"Mind yours, crone." Replied a frazzled Vanessa.

The lady scoffed, "I'm going to tell his mother."

"Fuck off!" said Vanessa, before slamming the door behind her.

Exasperated by what had just occurred, Vanessa dead bolted the door, leaned back onto it, and caught her breath.

"I want my mommy!" cried Oliver.

She then, picked him up, brought him into the kitchen, and put him into his high chair. Strapping him tightly, so he wouldn't fall out. She then wrapped his hands around the milk bottle and mushed it into his mouth. Oliver spit it out and threw the bottle on the floor, spattering milk all over Vanessa's jeans. Fraught with anger, she stood there clueless about what to do next. Glancing around the kitchen, she tried to think of something that might be useful, to quiet the little beast.

First, she rummaged through Oliver's bedroom, in an attempt to find a toy, or something that would help, calm him down. Then, she went into Carol's bedroom, but found nothing. Desperate to pacify young Oliver, Vanessa went into Carol's private bathroom. Where she opened the medicine cabinet. There, she was astounded by the array of anti-depressants, muscle relaxers, painkillers, and sleeping aids.

"Bloody 'ell, this woman's an addict." She said, out loud.

Vanessa picked up a bottle, shook it to see if there was anything left. It rattled like a baby's toy. She read the label to see what was. Proxycotine a powerful opioid, used to help bone cancer patients deal with pain. Vanessa's paused and stared at the bottle for moment. Suddenly, a familiar feeling came over her. A feeling she hadn't had, since she lived in London. Then, in an instant, a flashback of her, sticking a needle in her arm went through her head. She shook her head, placed the bottle back, and picked up another pill bottle. This time it was Tambian, a powerful sleep inducer that could knock out an adult in minutes. She paused again and thought about the ramifications, of drugging a child. But, normal adult reasoning prevailed. *I shouldn't be doing this. He's a child for god's sake.*

All of the sudden, the sound of glass shattering came from the dining room. Oliver had escaped again. She rushed back to the dining room to find a broken vase on the floor and a frightened little Oliver sobbing underneath the dining room table. His clothes were soaked, with water, sweat, and tears. *No blood, thank god.* Vanessa slowly approached him, trying not to upset him even more.

She crouches down to his level, "Hey Ollie, there you are. It's okay, are you hurt? I'm not mad. Nessa won't hurt you. Why don't you come out from under there?" She asked, talking to him in a calm and soothing tone. "You have got to be thirsty, I have your bottle. Here take it."

Oliver sat there whimpering, staring at her with a look of distrust on his face. Vanessa moved the chair out the way so she could get a better look at him. She placed the bottle down on the table, got on her hands and knees, and crawled slowly toward Oliver.

"Well come on ol' boy, let's get a bloody look at you."

Vanessa reached out her hand, in the hopes that he would trust her enough to take it, and come out from under the table.

Suddenly, Oliver shouted "No!"

Then, with a single back swing of his little arm, Oliver slashed Vanessa's finger with a piece of glass from the broken vase. She howled in pain, clutching her hand. Blood immediately began to pool on the tip of her finger. She stuck her finger in her mouth to stop the bleeding.

"You little shit!" She screamed.

Vanessa rushed back to the bathroom, grabbed the sleeping pills from the medicine cabinet, broke apart one of the capsules, and poured some of it into Oliver's baby bottle. When she returned, Vanessa yanked Oliver out from under the table. He shrieked at the top of his lungs while she held him down, prying his mouth open with one hand. Then grabbing the bottle and holding it over his head with the other hand. She poured the mixture of milk and Tambian into his mouth, as he struggled, spat, and coughed. Milk shot out of his little nose getting everywhere. Finally, she covered his mouth tightly, until he was forced to swallow. She kept him pinned down, waiting for the drug to take effect.

An hour later, Vanessa and a drowsy Oliver arrived at the Grand for his 9am, "Bach and Roll for Tots" children's music class. Vanessa was instantly awe struck, by The Grand's beauty and elegance. She couldn't believe such a place even existed. *I could get used to a place this.*

They headed upstairs to the Kiddies Only Area, where the class was. She unbuckled him from the stroller, picked up his limp little body, and put him in the drum circle. Where, all the other children and their nannies sat. She had to prop him up, so he wouldn't fall on his face.

"There you go Ollie, sit up nice and tall, so the teacher can see you." She said.

A teacher's aide came over. "Hey Oliver, we thought you weren't going to make it class today."

Oliver began nodding off. "Aw. Who's a little sleepy head? It's Oliver! Who's a little sleepy head? It's Oliver!" The teacher's aide sang.

"Yeah. He just woke up." Vanessa said. "He's still a little...groggy. A little music should fix that. Could you hold him for a sec?"

She handed Oliver over to the aide, got up, and headed for the exit. "I need to go to the loo, be back in a New York minute, thanks."

"Uh okay. We'll be right here, I guess." Said the aide.

Vanessa walked out of the playroom, leaving a barely conscious Oliver, with the teacher. She immediately found the ladies room, but walked right past it. Instead, she stepped onto the elevator and pressed the fitness floor button. As the elevator approached the gym floor, the faint sound of music, grew louder. When the elevator doors opened, she stepped out. Her eyes widened and her jaw dropped. *This is spectacular!*

Vanessa stood there taking it all in, as two gym members happened to walk by, with towels around their shoulders. One of the members wiped the sweat from his brow, and directed his friend toward the Lat Pull-down Machine. She followed them to see where they were going. She walked behind them, until they passed the studio, where a bootcamp class was in session. Vanessa stopped to for a moment to watch. The instructor was a short, stocky, muscular guy, demonstrating each of the exercises. He barked out orders, yelling above the loud music, and shouted in people's faces, when he thought they weren't giving him a hundred percent.

"What is this? You call that a pushup!" He yelled.

Vanessa's hand pressed up on the glass, her breath fogging it up, as she leaned in. The instructor looked up at her, winked, and smiled. She blushed a little and continued on her way, wandering around the gym floor. Eventually, she found herself by the free weights. Her hand glided across the shiny dumb bells, until she reached the end of the rack. Where tall muscular man, walked up next to her, and picked up the eighty-pound set of dumbells. She stood back and watched him lift the weights over his body. Exhaling forcefully every time he pressed them up toward the ceiling. Pre-occupied by this display of strength, she continued to watch as he completed he completed his first set. All of the sudden, she remembered the music class. *Holy shit, Oliver!*

Vanessa rushed back to the playroom. Parents and other caregivers had already put their children into their strollers, waving bye-bye to the class teacher. The aide, who'd been watching Oliver, approached Vanessa.

"Um hi, you've been gone awhile. You're really not supposed leave the children. This is an interactive class, where parents and care-givers are supposed to participate." Said the teacher unhappily.

"I am truly sorry, I got lost looking for the bathroom." Said Vanessa.

"Okay, well that happens, but just to let you know. I'm concerned that Oliver, is not feeling well."

They both looked over at Oliver, who was passed out, lying face down on the floor. A little girl was nearby, bouncing a ball off his head.

"He looks fine to me." Said Vanessa.

"Are you sure?"

"Of course, I'm sure." Vanessa paused. "I'm not one to talk, but since we're both professionals, in the field of childcare. I can trust you right?"

"Of course, you can." Said the aide.

"The problem is his mother, she's a pill addict, who has these late night parties. Men come in and out of the house, at all hours of the night, doing god knows what." Vanessa said, gesturing toward her nostril, implying cocaine use.

"Oh my god!" said the mortified teacher.

"Poor boy is traumatized by everything he's been exposed to. How can he sleep, what with all the orgies every night? And the worst part is that his mother is the only female."

"Oh my God!" The teacher was aghast.

"God! Oh no dear. Our God wouldn't allow this helpless little boy to be put through something so dreadful. She's the devil"

7

Boys Night Out

"What did you say your name was?" Asked the bouncer at the door, scrolling down his clipboard, with a yellow highlighter.

"Yeah um... Jason Garcia, G. A. R.—"

"Nope, don't see it. Step aside please." said the bouncer, looking up at the people behind Jason.

"Are you sure, my name's not on there?" Jason said. "Check the V.I.P. section, it's *got* to be there."

Jason texted Matt, *"Dude I'm outside, where u at!?"*

The bouncer skimmed his clipboard, for a third time. "I'm telling you, it's not on here."

Jason sighed. "Alright then, where's the line?"

"There is no line, this is a private party, " Said the bouncer, un-clasping the red velvet rope, to let in a well-dressed man sporting a bright, red faux-hawk and his date, a petite, but muscular woman, with long hair extensions on the left side of her head, and the hair completely shaved off on the right side.

"Really! Whose party is it?" Jason asked, curiously.

"Can't tell you that," Said the bouncer, scouring the crowd. "Stand aside, can't block the sidewalk."

"Well then, can I at least go see if my friends are inside?" Jason pleaded.

"Sorry can't do that, step *back* please."

Jason was stranded, outside of SauZae, a popular nightclub. Voted the city's most lit, new spot by Club Life Magazine. He waited impatiently, to hear back from Matt or Tommy, who were already inside, drinking and gawking at women. The streets were teeming with club goers, tourists, and locals. Looking to dance, drink, and possibly get lucky. SauZae itself was located at the heart, of the Meat Packing District, fashion mecca of the world. And, Jason

Garcia had somehow run aground alone, pondering his next move.

Suddenly, Matt peeked out, from behind the door. He stepped out, with Tommy right behind. Jason was so relieved that his boys had arrived. *Now what bitches.*

He waved to them, from behind the red velvet rope.

"It's about time! My name's not on the list." Jason shouted.

"Don't worry, we got this." Tommy shouted back.

Jason watched intently, as Matt whispered something into the bouncer's ear. He expected the hulking man, who stood almost a full foot over Matt, to come over and unclasp the red velvet rope. But, the bouncer shook his head again, no.

He told Matt and Tommy the same thing, he told Jason. "Step aside please."

Matt looked over at Jason, with a look of disappointment on his face. "I told him you're supposed to be on the guest list." Matt said. "I don't know what happened."

"Fuck, okay. So now what?" Jason asked, as people pushed past him.

Matt stood there for a moment, trying to figure out a solution. "Well… I'm not speaking for Tommy." Matt winced, preparing to sting Jason, "But I think, I'm going stay."

Tommy nodded in agreement, "Yeah, me too."

"Oh! So now you're *ditching* me?" Jason hollered, in disbelief.

The Bouncer turned to Matt and Tommy. "C'mon guys, either go in, or stay out. Can't block the entrance."

"Aw man. It's a *private* party. Normally, I would roll out with you," Matt explained, "but you have to understand, there are legit super models, up in here. You get what I mean dawg?"

"It's, it's a private party, Jay," Stammered Tommy.

"Last time guys, in or out." The Bouncer said impatiently.

"Okay, okay we're going." Said Matt.

He looked back at Jason, gave him a little shrug, as if to say he did everything he could. Tommy gave Jason one last wave goodbye, before they both turned around and headed back in. Deserting their brother in arms, leaving him outside alone to fend for himself.

Jason shook his head in disappointment. *Those assholes really ditched me!* He stood there by himself, jostled by all the pedestrians walking by. Down but not defeated, he looked around to see what else he could do. He was about to step off the curb, when a black SUV pulled up. He quickly stepped back. The front doors of the small truck opened and two men stepped out. One man dressed in an Italian suit, flashed a watch worth about eighteen thousand dollars, checked to see what time it was, while taking his ticket from the valet. The man on the passenger side wore fitted designer jeans, a button down shirt, with a gold chain around his neck. He went to open the rear door. Three very tall women stepped out, holding small, but very expensive purses. The tallest of the women, walked toward the velvet rope. Dumbfounded by the woman's height, Jason stepped off to the side, watching her as she approached.

She called out to the bouncer. "Jeremy!" she said, with a subtle Israeli accent.

The bouncer looked up and saw the woman waving. "Oh my God! Glenny, is that you?"

He rushed over, gave her a big hug, and kiss on the cheek.

"This is Jeremy, everybody. He used do security for me, back in the day. Although, I think you've lost weight. I think this job is getting to you. " She said kiddingly. "Jeremy this is my boyfriend, Nikolo, and this is my…"

She began to point out everybody in her crew, letting the bouncer know who was in the group. Instantly, Jason saw an opportunity. He turned around, quickly pulled out his cell phone and pretended to talk on it. With his back turn toward them, he slowly backed into the group.

"We are here for two days, then I fly back to Milan for a shoot," Glenny said, to Jeremy.

Jason carefully positioned himself furthest away from the bouncer. Just close enough, to blend in with the group, but not so close that the group noticed him. Jeremy unclasped the red velvet rope, while chatting with Glenny. Her entourage thanked Jeremy, as they walked past, shaking his hand and patting him on the shoulder.

"Yeah, I got that thing for you. It's in my Ferrari." Jason said, faking a conversation on the phone; Inconspicuously walking past

Jeremy, right into Glenny's friend Allegra; a tall, redhead, with luminous green eyes. Dotted with a small beauty mark on her lower right cheek. She looked down at Jason, confused.

Jason quickly spoke, before she could say anything. "Uh da um," He stammered. "Lovely evening we're having. Welcome to SauZae, I know what you're thinking, but no need to worry, your table is being set up, right as we speak."

Jason looked around, hoping he had remained undetected. Luckily nobody noticed, as he made his way into to the club.

Inside, Matt was throwing back a shot of tequila, while Tommy bit into a Lemon.

His face contorted "Ah! Rocket fuel." He said.

Jason walked up behind them. "Well, well look at this, my two good buddies, having a drink. All torn up by the fact, they *ditch*, a fellow comrade. How's that feel going down Tom?" Jason said, venomously.

"Hey! You made it in." Said Matt, applauding.

"Fuck you!" snapped Jason.

"Dude, the bouncer wasn't going to let you in, and he was gonna kick us out, if we didn't stop bothering him" Tommy explained.

"Fuck that shit, you guys ditched me… me!" Jason exclaimed.

"Oh yeah, take a look around, when's the last time you been to a party, with this many hot chicks? You would've dropped us like a hot potato, if we couldn't get in." said Matt.

"That is not true, I would've figured out a way to get everybody in. Except for Tommy, you're an asshole." He said distracted by Allegra, who was getting a drink, at the other end of the bar.

Jason winked at her, she sneered.

"Wait, what did I do?" replied Tommy.

"You know what, shut up and buy me a drink, we'll call it even."

"Yeah! That's what I'm talking about." Matt shouted, raising his shot glass.

"Another round please." said Tommy, signaling the bartender.

Tommy, Matt, and Jason all grabbed their drinks as they began to make their way through the club. SauZae itself was in an old Turkish bathhouse, converted into a nightclub, about ten years earlier. Back then it was called, Flux. It opened to great reviews and remained a very popular night spot, for about three years. Until the Feds shut it down, when it was discovered, the polish mob used it for money laundering. Ten months later, it reopened as Lit, only to get shut again, after someone was shot in the VIP section, for accidentally knocking over a drink. The Polish mob, was again investigated. But, no one was ever arrested, because no one would dare snitch.

The guys carefully maneuvered, onto the dance floor, holding their glasses in the air, weaving their way through the dancing crowd, hoping to catch the smile of a beautiful woman.

Jason followed closely, as Matt parted the dance floor, like an ice cutter ship in the Arctic Circle slicing through a sea of hot, sweaty people. Tommy lagged behind, unable to keep up. Because he had to talk, to every girl he passed. Eventually, they circled back to the bar, as if it were some home base where they could regroup before the next patrol. Jason put his drink down at a table, with some stools that had recently been vacated.

Maybe, it was the alcohol taking effect, or the large blunt he smoked, before the club. But, Jason became more and more preoccupied, by the day's earlier events, with Vanessa. He replayed the whole thing in his mind, trying to understand the situation. Except this time, she was topless. For some reason, it helped take the sting out of her words. *She's making me responsible, for their livelihood. What kind of fiendish shit is that!*

"Yo Jay, you drunk man, you seem quiet?" Matt asked.

"No I was just thinking about something that happened today." Jason replied.

"Have you guys noticed anything different, with Vanessa lately?" He asked, taking a drink from his glass.

"No she seems normal to me," said Tommy. "And by normal, I mean she'll pull your scrotum over your head, if you look at her wrong, normal. Why do you ask, is something amiss?"

"I'm not sure. She seems more agitated than usual." Jason replied. "Something's up. By the way, you sound like a gay Musketeer. Is something amiss."

"As opposed to a straight Musketeer." Tommy laughed. "Seriously though, you think something's up, with Vanessa?"

"I'm not sure, but are you implying all Musketeers are gay? Because, I don't think Musketeer's would appreciate it. Anyway, today at work, Vanessa really let me have it."

Tommy took a sip of his drink. "What did she tickle your throat, with her lady-boy dick?"

"Can't say lady boy dick anymore, hashtag love wins, remember?" Matt interrupted.

"Oh jeez, you think anyone heard me?" Tommy said, anxiously looking around.

Jason sighed, taking another sip. "She threatened to fire us, if we didn't generate more revenue, for the fitness department."

"Wait, what?" Tommy exclaimed. "What do you mean us?"

"Us! You know, me, you, Matt, maybe Bex. Who knows? " Jason said.

"Whoa, whoa, whoa hold the *motherfucking* phone." Said Tommy, trying to comprehend.

"Hold the motherfuck—what are you, the Chinese Sam Jackson now?" Said Jason.

Tommy turned to Matt, "Matt, you know about this?"

"What?" Matt yelled.

"Vanessa is going to fire everybody, if we don't start bringing in more money." Tommy said, turning back to Jason, "Is that even legal?"

"Does it matter if its legal, we're talking about Vanessa here." Jason said, chugging his beer.

Matt smacked his lips. "Man that bitch, ain't gonna do *shit*. She still mad at Jay, for rejecting her a hundred years ago, that's all... """

"That's what I thought too, but this is different. I think corporate might have something to do with it." Jason said.

"*Motherfucking* corporate! Why?" Tommy yelled.

"Not sure, drunk *Samu-el*, but she seemed bothered, right after talking to that guy from corporate during the party the other night. What was that guy's name?" Jason snapped his fingers, trying to remember. "It's something Richards. Anyway, I bet your mother's sweet virgin asshole. That's what set her off."

Matt laughed. "At least someone's asshole is still virgin." Referring to an incident between Jason and Vanessa.

"Touché pussy cat." Jason laughed, holding up his glass. "Thomas Richards! That's the guy's name, at the Halloween party. I heard he was pissed when Vanessa was promoted to GM.

"Oh yeah… Carla was his girl right?" Matt said, "Everybody was so distraught about her accident, but he *really* took it bad. Was he fucking her? Shit I would've."

Jason wondered, "Maybe… He did make a big fuss, about Vanessa though. Bex, told me that Richards suspects, Vanessa was behind the accident."

Matt and Tommy both paused, for a moment.

"Come on Jay, you really believe Vanessa had something to do with Carla, driving her car into the Hudson River?"

"It came from Bex, she trained him, until Vanessa became GM. She said he couldn't stand, being around her. Can't say I blame him, she is tough. "

"So Vanessa's a homicidal maniac, bent on ruling The Grand?" Matt asked.

They all paused for a beat, then laughed at the thought.

"But you think Fit Corp, is making another play for The Grand?" Tommy asked, while leering at a woman walking past.

"Makes sense, they're the ones with the deepest pockets." Jason said. "Haven't you noticed how they've been expanding into every major city in the country, for the past couple of years? They're literally buying up the competition."

"She can't really fire all of us." Tommy said, turning back to Jason.

"Trust me, my little dumpling. If Vanessa wants you gone, she'll find a way." "Well then…" Matt said, "…we need to figure some shit out, because I cannot lose my job over some *bullshit!* There is no way I'll make the same money somewhere else. I'll have to leave the city."

"This is bad, real bad," said Tommy, becoming increasingly concerned. "If I lose my job, I'll have to move back home. Then my parents will know I dropped out of medical school."

Matt laughed, "Tiger Mom's going to one-inch punch you in the throat, huh?"

"Not funny, dick!" Tommy replied, punching Matt in the arm.

"Look there's no need to worry," said Jason. "All we have to do is get more clients. How hard can that be, the economy *is* coming back, right?" *Or am I, just fooling myself?*

"Can we *please* change the subject, for a moment." Matt interjected, "I'm tired of being all serious 'n shit. Especially, when there's so much *ass* around here. Look at that over there!"

Matt pointed over to two women in the V.I.P. area, dancing seductively, with each other.

Tommy and Jason both looked over. "*Damn...*" they said, in unison.

The straw from Tommy's drink fell out of his mouth. His glazed eyes widened, transfixing, on the grinding beauties. The beat of the music, pounded hard and loud. As if it was in sync with the thudding of his heart. The bright, colorful disco lights spun, whirled, and flashed across the room, disorienting him. The strobe lights flashed across their bodies, making the movements of the women, look hypnotic. By this point, Tommy was so drunk, his conscious mind had completely handed the reigns over to his reptilian brain.

At first, Tommy just stood there leaning on the bar, leering with lustful intent.

Envisioning their sweating, naked bodies intertwined with his. He stiffened his legs, stood up straight, and mustered up enough liquid courage, to go talk to them. He became so single minded, so intent on getting to that V.I.P. area. That he hadn't noticed, stepping onto the dance floor. Bumping and jostling, people as they danced. He stalked over like a creepy, drunken lion in the Serengeti. Ready to pounce on two full-grown elephants. He didn't have a chance in hell, but he circled them nonetheless. His face had become flush and bright, from all the drinking. To his ears, the music sounded distant, almost muffled.

Everyone around him seemed to be moving in slow motion, staring at him, as they nudged their friends: *look at that fucked up dude, on the dance floor.*

Tommy's tongue searched around for the straw, in his drink. His lips pulled it into his mouth. Ogling the women passionately dancing with one another, from across the dance floor. *Me want touchy.*

"That's the hottest Asian chick I've ever seen." Matt said, transfixed.

"I think you might be right this time, although we stopped calling women, chicks a long time ago." Jason remarked. "That blonde though, damn! What was my point? Anyway, where did Tommy go?"

The two girls got closer, their lips within millimeters of kissing, daring the other to make a move. The Blonde was tall and lean. She wore a short, black, sparkly dress, fitted with the iconic red-soled, six-inch heels. Her skirt slid up her long, glistening thighs, as she grinded on her dance partner.

All of the sudden, the sound of glass breaking, rang out over the music. The women were spattered, with cranberry juice and cheap vodka.

"Oh sorry, don't mind me ladies. That was awesome don't stop, on my account. I'm cool." Tommy said, sitting down across from them. "Here, let me get that for you."

He attempted to wipe, the spilled drink off one their dresses.

"Oh my god, ewe! This guy is so creepy." The Blonde said. "Let's go."

"No wait! Let me help you." Tommy said, desperately stumbling after them, pointing his finger at them, so as to not lose them in the crowd.

"Okay Tommy boy, we're calling a time out." Matt said, as he walked over putting his hand on Tommy's shoulder.

"You alright man? How many drinks did you have?" Jason asked.

"He had two, I was counting." Matt replied.

"Two drinks, that's it?"

"He's got that Asian-alcohol thing going on." Matt said, "He can't process the booze correctly, so his body has what looks an allergic reaction. Sometimes he gets this red flush in his face, other times he needs to sleep, but tonight Tommy's becomes a serial pervert."

"That apparently masturbates in public," said Jason, noticing Tommy's hand in his pocket, playing with himself.

"Huh? Oh! C'mon man!" Matt said, taking his hand off Tommy. "What's wrong with you!"

"We need to sit him down, before he gets kicked out." Jason said, scanning the room. They headed back to the bar, to get Tommy some water.

"Hey, you okay man, cause this is some next level?" Matt asked.

"I'm super fine," Tommy slurred. "Just get me back on the dance floor, cause I'm about to be like… like… LeBron, and dunk on these bitches."

"That makes no sense." Said Jason.

Matt signaled the bartender, "Can we get some water, for our friend?"

"I brought my A-game, to this wack ass party. These 'hoes need to be woke!" Tommy said, starting to slip off his stool.

Jason quickly grabbed him, propping him back up. "Oh boy, we're losing him," he said, concerned.

Matt handed, Tommy a bottled water. "A little bit for me," said Tommy, taking a sip, from the bottle. "And a little bit, for my dead homies."

He then, pours the rest water on the floor. "Tupaaaac!"

"Tommy no…" Jason Said.

"Not good, not good." Matt added.

Tommy then takes the empty water bottle and punts it across the club into the crowd. "NOTORIOUS!!!"

Jason and Matt cringed, looking to see if anyone had even noticed.

"Ha ha, try to punt return that Matt." Tommy joked.

"This dude is turnt up, to eleven. You're gonna get us kicked out." Matt said, trying not to draw attention to them.

"*Shiiiit.* They ain't kicking me out, cause I'm about to serve, somebody up in this bitch." Tommy said, attempting to break dance on the floor.

Jason turned to Matt "Maybe we let him get kicked out. I'd love to see the look on his face, when they grab him."

Suddenly, as if out of nowhere, a plastic water bottle smacked Tommy, right in the face. A man about average height, covered in tattoos, stepped out from the crowd. His ears were scarred up and swollen, resembling pieces of cauliflower. Stood there glaring, at Tommy.

"Wanna tell me why my girl got hit in the face, with your fucking bottle?" The man demanded.

Tommy's eyes began to re-focus, as he slowly started coming out, of his belligerent haze. He slowly realized, who was standing in front him.

First, there was a look of innocent disbelief. *Wait... did I just piss off Crazy Mike Thorpe?* Immediately, a look of pure terror came over him.

"Oh shit, that's that ultimate fighter dude." Matt said, in amazement.

"Who?" Jason asked, trying to get a better look.

"That's Crazy Mike Thorpe, the middle weight champ." Matt replied. "Fuck man, we need to get out of here now. That guy's unstable. "

"Ah yeah... well you look at that... it is Crazy Mike, hmm... he's so much shorter in person." Jason said, not really grasping the situation.

"Dude, you don't understand, he's going to kill Tommy." Matt said. "My client is a fight promoter and he told me that one time. After beating the crap out of an opponent, he went to his house and smacked his parents for giving birth to him. Then he smacked the family dog... the dog Jay."

"What! C'mon man, he didn't do that."

Matt gave Jason a sideways stare, "Trust me, my client knows a guy that knows Crazy Mike, from back in the day. We don't wanna fuck, with this dude."

Crazy Mike stepped up to Tommy. "Who let you into my party?"

"Oh I'm sorry, Mike sir. I didn't know this was your party." Tommy said, apologetically.

"How'd you get in?" He demanded, looking Tommy up and down.

"Look um... I'm just here, with some friends." Tommy said, trying to explain the situation. "I didn't realize that this was—"

"What friends?"

"My... my... my friends." Tommy stammered, pointing to toward the spot. Where, Jason and Matt had been standing, a split second ago. *Fist me in the ass!*

"I don't appreciate people crashing my party," said Crazy Mike, clenching his jaw, drawing even closer to Tommy.

"But, I was on the guest list." Tommy said.

"I don't give a fuck, what the guest list says." He said, cracking his neck, circling Tommy. "I don't know you, motherfucker."

"You're right, of course. I should just go, it's getting late, and I have to be at work early. I'm sorry for crashing your party. Won't happen again, Mr. Crazy Mike."

"What… all this trouble for you to get in. Now you want to leave? You just hurt my feelings," Crazy Mike said, menacingly. "But you are right, it is getting late."

Crazy Mike took a big swig, from his whiskey bottle, and wiped the excess from his chin. He then grabbed Tommy, above the elbow. "So let me show you out."

Crazy Mike pulled Tommy, toward a rear exit. "Wait, wait, the door's this way," Tommy said, trying to resist.

Crazy Mike escorted, Tommy away. Suddenly, the music stopped and the stage lights came on.

"Test, test, one, two, one, two…"

It was Jason, coming out from behind the DJ booth, tapping the microphone.

"Alright, alright! Ladies and gentlemen, let me hear you make some noise! Welcome to SauZae, New York City's premiere night-club. Is everybody here having a good time?"

The crowd cheered.

"I can't hear you! Is everybody having a good time tonight???"

The crowd cheered even louder.

"Yes! That's what I'm talking about," Jason yelled, getting the crowd pumped. "So without further ado, let's bring up the guest of honor. He's a badass in the ring, a new middleweight champion of the world, and our birthday boy. Let's hear it for, Crazy Mike Thorpe!"

The spotlight shined on Crazy Mike, who still had Tommy, by the arm, when he realized, all the attention was on him.

"Come up and say a few words Mike." Jason said, trying to draw his attention, away from Tommy.

The crowd chanted, *Crazy! Crazy! Crazy!* Jason began to sing "Eye of the Tiger." Crazy Mike hesitated for a second, before releasing Tommy, and heading for the stage.

"That's it! Mike, say a few words, to the people that love you. Everybody hold up your glasses, for Crazy Mike's toast. Eh... can we get a glass for Mr. Crazy here?" Jason asked.

Matt came up to the stage, holding three shot glasses, passing one to Jason and one to Crazy Mike.

Jason passed the microphone to Crazy Mike, who stood there squinting in the bright lights, not really sure what to say.

"Uh, thank you all for coming to my party. It's uh, an honor... to have you'se out here for me. So uh, let's fucking party!" Crazy Mike shouted, raising his glass.

Jason grabbed the microphone. "You heard the man. Cheers! Let's fucking party!!!" The crowd screamed. "DJ, let's get this party tight!"

The music came back on, and the crowd went wild.

"I told Jason we'd meet him outside." Matt said, rushing past Tommy. "Let's get the fuck out of here, before Crazy Mike decides, to kill us too." Tommy took one last look around the room, taking in the hot girls, before following Matt out the front door.

8

Happy Ending

It had been six months, since Vanessa intentionally drugged, 3 year old, Oliver Hudson: And six months since, someone anonymously called child services, on his mother Carol. Vanessa decided that her days of babysitting snot-nosed, little, brats were over. Instead, she took a job as a spa receptionist, in The Grand's beautiful, wellness spa.

Vanessa worked six days a week, ten hours a day. Not only did she answer phones and schedule appointments. She also folded towels and made sure all of the treatment rooms, were fully stocked. She didn't mind the work—she was good at it—and anything was better, than changing shitty diapers, all day long.

However, there were parts of the job that Vanessa had quickly become dissatisfied with. It was utterly brainless, and she resented having to do all the grunt work, while being treated badly; or ignored entirely, by members. She would watch the massage therapists, enviously, as they came and went, as they pleased. In charge of their own schedules, getting treated with respect. Sometimes they received lavish gifts, get taken out to fancy restaurants, and meet very interesting people through their clientele. Vanessa wanted that for herself. Determined to get ahead, she saved for several months in order to finally be able to apply, to the Finnish Institute of Massage.

Vanessa spent the next two years working reception at the Grand during the day in order, to pay for school at night. Every waking hour of her life was dedicated to her dream of making a better life for herself. To become part of the glamorous, New York culture that the Grand embodied for her. Her love life was dead on arrival. She spent what little money she made, on her Lower East Side apartment. She was barely able to afford a cell phone but she persevered, despite her circumstance. *Be patient, it'll pay off.*

One evening during a grueling study session, Vanessa received a notification from an email account she hadn't used in years. From someone she hadn't seen in years, someone she thought was dead.

"... Bloody 'ell" she said out loud as her heart skipped a beat. She immediately clicked on the notification button to make sure she wasn't imagining things.

"Hello V, long time... -Love, M." She leaned back in shock.

Another notification popped up, she clicked on it.

"How is New York City?"

Vanessa, abruptly closed the laptop, and went to the window. The hairs on the back of her neck stood up as she looked out. A feeling of dread came over her, a feeling she hadn't felt in a long time.

The street was quiet, except for a green taxi passing by, and a young woman with her dog sitting up against the building, on the other side of the street. She held out a cup, asking for money. The dog sat obediently next to her, while she held up a sign that said. "I'm homeless, please help me feed my dog."

Vanessa sat back down in her chair, wondering. *Maxwell but how...*

She poured herself a shot of whiskey and stared at the email for a long time. *How does he know where I am?* Vanessa shuddered of the thought of this Maxwell coming back into her life.

The year was 2008, and Vanessa had finally finished massage school. She felt her dreams were finally within reach, but in order for her to make money, she needed clients. She devised an ambitious plan, to get clients at The Grand. First, she would give fifteen-minute chair massages, to members on the fitness floor and hopefully convince them to purchase full sessions after. Second, she would exploit her femininity by wearing revealing clothes during her workouts, in order to get the attention of male members with disposable income. Playing off their attraction to her, charming them into booking massage sessions. Finally, she would talk to the personal trainers and offer them a deal; Free massages in exchange for trainers referring their clients exclusively to her. *That'll definitely keep me in business.*

One afternoon Jason Garcia, who had been working as a trainer at the Grand for about two years, went down to the café to grab a protein shake, after a particularly grueling workout. While waiting for his order, he noticed Vanessa, who also happened to be waiting in line.

"Wow how long does it take to make a protein shake, what are they milking the cow back there?" Jason said, trying to strike up a conversation.

"I wouldn't know. I don't drink dairy," replied Vanessa.

"Really? Why is that?" Jason asked.

"Because it makes you fat and causes cancer."

"What! I never heard that. And here I thought, I was feeding my muscles." Jason joked, trying to read Vanessa's response. "My name is Jason, I'm a trainer here."

"I know who you are." Vanessa said.

"Oh well then, I guess my reputation precedes me. How 'bout that? So you're new here, or what?"

"No. I've been working in the spa for two years."

"Wow really? Shows how much I know about the spa huh?"

Jason's Killer Gains Protein Shake came up at the same time, as Vanessa's Green Power juice. Jason motioned toward a table, seeing if Vanessa wanted to continue the conversation. She nodded and walked over to sit down.

"So what do you do that's keeps you so busy?" Jason asked.

"Nothing," she said, looking at him strangely.

"Nothing! Well that's good right? Getting paid to do nothing." He said. "I'd be awesome at that."

"Not really," she said, "you get treated like a "nobody". You're invisible most of the time, and no one appreciates what you do. But that's all been different, since I got my massage license."

"Well that's great, congratulations… cheers!" Jason said, holding up his protein shake. "You know come to think of it, I've been working here a little more than a year, and I've never gotten a massage."

"How appalling." Vanessa said, cracking a smile.

"I know right." He said, slurping his shake.

Vanessa leaned forward in her seat, ready to pitch her idea "Well then, since you mentioned it. I have been talking to some of the trainers… I told them that I would give them free massages in exchange for client referrals. That way, they know exactly what I do. So if any of their clients, ask about who gives the best massages here, they know to whom they should refer."

Jason smiled. "Hm. I've been looking for a Masseuse, how good are you?"

Vanessa rolled her eyes, "It's *Massage Therapist*… And I'm extremely thorough."

"Okay I'm sold, when do you want to start?" Jason asked, trying to read the situation. "By the way, do you give happy endings?"

"Excuse me?" Vanessa asked, taken aback.

Aware of her tone, Jason laughed, trying to play it off as a joke. "Ha ha never mind, just messing with you." *But not really…*

"I gotta admit I'm excited, this is gonna be awesome." Jason slurped the last of his protein shake. "Hey, I'll tell you what, if you give me a couple a massages, here and there. I'll train you."

Vanessa took a sip of her green juice and looked Jason up and down. *He's actually pretty cute, even if he's dumb as fuck.*

"Sounds like a deal." She said.

Jason and Vanessa shook hands, agreeing to exchange services. Jason would train Vanessa, getting her into fabulous shape and in return, she would give him relaxing back rubs. The two worked well together. They referred each other business and both made a lot of money. Things appeared to be going smoothly and Vanessa was pleased with her decision. Very quickly, she became one of the highest earning massage therapists at the Grand, catching the attention and earning the respect of management. Jason also did his part by, talking her up to the other trainers, who became interested in striking similar bargains. After a few months, Vanessa finally felt like she was starting to live the life she wanted for herself.

A year later, on a rainy spring evening a group of The Grand's employees were going out for drinks. Vanessa showed up alone, having been invited by Jason to join him and the crew at a local bar in SoHo. Everyone seemed to be chill and relaxed, as the stress of the week faded away. The jukebox played rock and roll music from the eighties and some of the girls were singing Bon Jovi's "Living on a Prayer" to each other while dancing in a circle with their high-heels kicked off and their handbags thrown on the floor. Most of the guys stood on the outskirts of the dance floor, watching them like prey, trying to muster the courage to make a move. The drinks kept coming and the music kept blaring. Vanessa and Jason stayed by the bar talking and laughing at each other's client horror stories.

Vanessa signaled the bartender for her twelfth drink. Jason stared in amazement, "Wow you really know how to drink. I am trashed." He said.

"That's because the drinks here are watered down, except their beer, I'm barely buzzed." She said.

"Damn and here I thought I'd get you so drunk, you'd let me take advantage of you. Looks like that back fired." He said, they both laughed.

"How do you know I'm not the one trying to get you drunk?" Vanessa said, devilishly.

"What do you mean... oh..." Jason asked, realizing what was really going on. Vanessa smiled finding his naïve stupidity refreshing after a week of listening to her massage clients complain about the stock market.

Flash forward, to four in the morning—as it always does, when one is enjoying the company of another. The bartender, a tall brunette dressed in a tight black cotton tank top that barely contained her breasts, began to close out the remaining open tabs.

"Last call for alcohol, you don't have to go home, but you can't stay here." She said, impatiently.

The sounds of empty beer bottles clanged together in the background, as the bar-backs took them out to the alley. The last remaining patrons finished up their drinks, counted out their cash, and left tips for the bartender; who was busy wiping down the bar, ignoring the futile attempts of a drunken slob hitting on her. The remaining people from The Grand put on their coats, walked out together, said their goodbyes and dispersed into various directions; drunkenly, making their way home. Most either flagged down cabs, or stumbled down into the subway.

Jason and Vanessa preferred to walk—it was only eight blocks to her house, and he had offered to walk her home. Everything except for a few delis were closed at that time of night and it was one of those few times when the city actually felt still and quiet, save the occasional drunken yell from a few blocks away. The streets were wet from a light rain earlier in the evening and there was a pleasing sound as cars drove down the street beside them, their tires almost sticking to the wet road. It was almost soothing, especially after being in a crowded bar all night. Jason was too drunk to really notice any of it, but Vanessa felt at ease and happy. It felt too soon to let it end when they arrived at Vanessa's place.

Jason looked around "So this is where you live? Nice spot. You have a deli… lucky!"

"Oh I hate that deli." Vanessa said, unlocking the door to the building. "I suppose this is where you say 'so I guess this is it' and tell me that it's been lovely and that you really should be going."

Jason stared blankly. He would never say anything like that.

Vanessa continued, "but I think what you really want is to come inside."

Jason tried drunkenly to play along. "How dare you make the assumption that I am some drunken hussy who wants to be taken advantage of? I am gravely offended. And what's more—"

"Are you coming in, or not?" Vanessa interrupted.

"Yeah I'd love to." Jason said, changing his tone and doing his best to stand up straight, not even attempting to be suave anymore

Vanessa grabbed Jason and started kissing him. He was sloppy but still a good kisser, and he was surprisingly tender. Vanessa pulled away. "I like you, Jason"

"I like me too." He said.

He kissed softly on her neck. Her heart beat loudly and her breath deepened.

She took his hand, leading him up the stairs, which creaked underneath their rushed footsteps. They stopped at the door to her apartment.

"This is very unlike me." She said, opening the door and walking into her studio.

"I never assumed it was like you. Being…um…un…like…you? Oh this is cozy." He said, referring to her studio, trying to save face.

Vanessa kissed him, and his hands grabbed her by the waist, lifting her up into the air. Her legs clutch his hips, as he carried her over to the bed, gently putting her down. Jason's could feel her hips gyrating in his hands, her heart racing as she spread her body out. He unbuttoned her blouse, her breasts heaved up and down. Vanessa un-tucked his shirt, and undid his belt with a snap. She reached eagerly into his boxer briefs. Jason quietly moaned with pleasure as she stroked him, getting him ready for what was about to happen. He pulled off her dress, leaving nothing but a tiny thong. He kissed, nibbled, and licked her starting from her breasts, down to her stomach, then making his way down between her thighs. All of the sudden she stiffened up, becoming rigid, Jason stopped.

"You okay?" He asked. "I have a condom."

"I'm fine, it's my turn." She replied.

"Its' in my pocket, let me get it." He said, while she bit his chin.

"You won't need that." She said.

"Uh… Don't you think… you know… since this is our first time… that we should?" He said, trying not to ruin the moment.

Vanessa stopped "Don't worry I'm going to give you the best orgasm of your life."

"Well in that case…"

"Good." She said

Vanessa rolled over and grabbed the coconut oil from a drawer in her nightstand.

"Oh okay… a little more foreplay… Keep things interesting." Jason said, watching her with anticipation.

"Something like that…" she said, rubbing the oil on her hands. "Have you ever heard of Lingam?"

"Lingam, no. Sounds kinky though." He said.

"It's the Tantric term for Shaft of Light." Vanessa continued. "An ancient East Indian method of pleasuring a man until he has multiple orgasms. Like the Kama Sutra"

"Mm… Like a Tantric Light saber," Jason tried to grasp the idea in vain. "I knew you were a freak in bed. I always know these things."

"You have no idea..." She replied, grinning devilishly from ear to ear, "But you're about to find out."

Vanessa began to massage the base of his shaft. Jason lay there looking up at the ceiling, wondering what this Lingam stuff is all about, trying to relax and enjoy the moment. Her strokes began to undulate, going from long and slow to a more circular motion with a tightening grip. He moaned and panted, grabbing the sheets like he was trying to tear them to shreds. *Shit, this is awesome!*

"Ooh... ah... hmm... whoa... I'm about to... ah..." Jason said, coming right to the edge.

"Shh, just breathe, control your energy."

Vanessa stopped right before Jason climaxed. "Are you ready?" she asked.

"Yes! My god, yes" He said, trying hard to catch his breath.

Suddenly, Vanessa flipped him onto his stomach, spreading his legs with her knees.

"Wha...what are you doing?" He asked, looking back at her.

"You ready to cum or not?" She asked forcefully.

"Ye... yeah but..."

Vanessa stuck her finger swiftly into Jason's anus.

Jason was startled, "No, I don't think, actually..." He said, trying to turn over.

Vanessa held him down with one hand, and felt around for his prostate with the other.

"There you go, old chap. Just relax. Shh."

"Oh god! This was not at all, what I was expecting... ahh!" He said, muffled by the pillows, "You are extraordinarily strong! Aye, aye, aye!"

"Shh... I almost...." Vanessa said, rooting around. *Got it!*

Jason howled as if he'd lost someone dear to him. He spasmed out and came all over himself, confused by an overwhelming mix of emotions. He pulled himself off the bed, falling to the floor. He crawled backward into the corner.

"What you just experienced was pure ecstasy, your mind and body became one with your soul, shedding you of all the egoistic and toxic feelings that bind you… I'm freeing you Jason."

Jason started sobbing. "You freed your finger into my ass for sure, I don't know about toxic ego whatever… so rude." Jason said.

"Don't you feel a sense of enlightenment? Free from all things superficial and the bound up energy inside you?" Vanessa asked.

"Hell no, but I'm definitely bound up now. I'm not going to be able to take a shit for a week!" Jason said, picking himself up from the floor, looking for his clothes. "How big are your hands? It felt like you were wearing a boxing glove."

"Hmm… Maybe I did it wrong." Vanessa said.

Jason wiped his eyes and grabbed his clothes from a pile on the floor.

"Baby, come over here, let me help you." Vanessa said, kneeling on her bed.

"No thank you." Jason said, gingerly putting on his pants.

"I don't understand, I thought we were having fun."

"Yeah… we were until you violated my no fly zone with your giant man hands."

Vanessa opened her palms, confused. *Man hands…*

"So I'm gonna go now." Jason patted his pockets, making sure he had got everything. "This was great fun—let's not do it again."

Vanessa got up, trying to explain herself "But…"

Jason backed up into a wall, "Stay back—I mean, please, don't get up."

"Don't you want to explore these feelings?" Vanessa said, placing her hands on his chest. "You need to explore these feelings, Jason. You have so much potential if you just let yourself be free of the patriarchy."

Jason trembled as he looked down at Vanessa's guilty finger on his chest. "Nah, I have a client in a couple of hours, I need to go." He said, almost bursting into tears. "Sorry"

Vanessa stood there confused, "We have a training session first thing tomorrow, remember?" she said, watching him grab the rest of his things.

He opened the door "Yeah, I'll see you tomorrow." He said, closing the door without looking back.

The next day Vanessa showed up early to her appointment with Jason. She stood by the fitness desk where she usual met him, eagerly waiting to talk to him about the night before. A couple of her clients walked by waving hello; she smiled and waved back, her mind wandering. Fifteen minutes went by, and Jason still hadn't arrived. She called him on his cell, but it went straight to voicemail.

"Hey, you've reached Jason Garcia's voicemail, I'm currently unavailable at the moment, probably because I'm busy getting someone into the best shape of their life, just kidding, but not really. Leave a message and I'll get back to you within 24hrs, thanks." The voicemail beeped.

"Oh Jason, Hi it's me, Vanessa… Look I hope you're still not sore at me… ha, no pun intended, just joshing. Anyway I'm here and you're not, so call me back, I guess. Let me know you're okay." Vanessa hung up and tried again, but it still went straight to voicemail. "It's me again… listen, Jason, I know you're not here because of last night. I'm sorry. I was really drunk and I usually don't behave like that. I just… Look, please call me back so we can talk about it. Jason, I really—" The voicemail beeped, cutting Vanessa off. Vanessa stood there for a minute, ambivalent about not being able to finished her admission. She realized Jason wasn't coming. Feeling a little hurt, a little like an idiot, and a little relieved, she walked off.

Just a few yards away, across the gym floor, Jason was hiding behind a plastic tree, watching Vanessa leave. He sighed in relief, got up, and dusted off his pants. He turned to go back to work, bumping straight into Vanessa who had come back around to look for him one more time.

"Oh God!" Jason yelped, falling to the ground. "How did you? I mean, I was just about to—"

"Save it Jay!" Vanessa said angrily. "You were just going to stand me up for some misunderstanding, and then not even talk to me."

"No, see, I was just about to call you back, and, and…" said Jason, scrambling for words.

"Bull shite Jay!"

"No you know what's bull*shite*? Getting an unsolicited finger banging in my butt-hole! That was completely uncalled for, not to mention rapey." Jason said.

Vanessa scoffs, "Rapey! How dare you! I am a respectable massage therapist, licensed by the good state of New York. I was only trying to enlighten you about the ancient art of the Kama Sutra, trying to help rid you of your backward, patriarchal mind."

"Yeah, but instead you bruised my ego, and more or less my prostate." Jason said, trying to squirm his way out of there. "I think we should stop hanging out for a while. I just can't be cool right now." He said. "Damn it, why do I feel like crying again?" He started tearing up.

"Fine! That's all you had to say. Instead you're just hiding out here like a bloody coward!"

"For your information, I was not hiding. I was simply trying to see if the tree needed water." Jason said, knocking on the tree. "It seems okay right now."

"The tree is plastic, you bloody idiot. Ugh!" Vanessa said exasperated, walking off in a huff. Jason stayed behind feeling the tree. *Plastic? It looks so real.*

Two days later, Vanessa was at the gym café to grab a bite to eat. She ordered an avocado salad and green tea. While, reaching into her purse to pull out her cash, she noticed Jason sitting at the other end of the café with Arnold, one of his clients. He and Jason were discussing Arnold's training program over a cup of coffee. Jason saw her waiting for her food and gave her a hello nod. Vanessa didn't acknowledge him back.

The clerk came back with Vanessa food, handed it to her and took her money, giving her the difference. She took the change, put it into her bag as she walked over to a table at the completely opposite end of the café and sat down. Calmly unfolding the napkin on her tray, she placed it neatly on her lap. Vanessa proceeded to drizzle a little balsamic vinegar on her crisp avocado salad. Then picking up a slice of lime and squeezed it over the salad until the lime stopped dripping. She then picked up her fork and began mashing the avocado into the shredded lettuce and baby tomatoes. Making sure the lime was evenly blended in.

Minutes later, Jason and Arnold got up. Jason threw his bag over his shoulder as they walked out. Jason slowed down and patted Arnold on the back, letting him know that he was going to stay behind. Arnold looked back, waved goodbye and left through the lobby. Jason turned around and headed to where Vanessa was sitting, watching her as she took another bite of her salad.

"Mind if I sit down?" Jason asked, standing at the other end of her table.

Vanessa took another bite without saying a word, looking through him as if he wasn't even there. "I'll... take that as no." said Jason, pulling out the chair and sitting down.

"Look Vanessa, I'm sorry about what I said the other day. I was overwhelmed and didn't know how to handle the situation. Instead, I acted like an asshole... no pun intended." He said, waiting for a reaction. Vanessa continued eating without reacting. Jason waved his hand in front of her face to get her attention.

"Oh I see. You're ignoring me. That's not immature at all." He said, sarcastically. "C'mon Vanessa, is this what you really want? Don't forget, *you* were the one that invaded my virgin butt-hole, without my consent to boot. Did you know I was constipated the next day, not cool." He said, still getting no response. Vanessa put down her tea, wiped her mouth, then picked up her fork and continued eating.

"Ok. If this is how you want it fine!" said Jason, picking his bag up off the floor. He pushed out his chair and got up, turning to walk away. He took five steps and turned back to Vanessa.

"You know it's very hard to be friends with someone who, like, won't even talk to you. You should be nicer to people who do things for you, like help you build your business. So... you're welcome."

Vanessa calmly put down her fork, picked up her napkin, and wiped her mouth. She got up from the table and walked over to Jason, looking deep into his eyes, as if she were about to punch him in the face. Jason braced himself.

"You must feel like really hot shite, don't ya? After all, you gave me so much business. I guess I should be more grateful, because without you, I'd be nothing. Is that right?" She said.

"That's not at all what I meant..." He said, trying to backtrack.

"No that's exactly what you meant. You actually thought that if you helped me get clients, that I would fuck you."

"Out of line! Vanessa, I wasn't trying to get into your pants. I was just trying to help you get started on the right foot here, that's all." He said, "You give me a massage, I train you. That was the agreement remember?"

"Really? Well let me tell you something, you bloody tosser. I am not one of your wretched slags, nor am I someone to fuck with. I've come too far to be distracted by some over-paid, adult nanny who counts *reps* for a living." She said, looking down at his gut. "And who can't seem to skip that fourth slice of pepperoni pizza!"

"Hey! I'm in a bulking phase," Jason said defensively, "besides its off season. You know, you should be careful with those *Bri'ish* insults. Someone's going to think you're complimenting them."

"Humph, don't ever underestimate a chav from the streets you wank. We can smell bull shite before you even open your mouth." Vanessa said, gathering her things.

"Now, who are you referring to? Because I'm confused and does this mean we're not training anymore?" He asked.

"It means you can stick it up your arse... pun intended." She answered back, sticking up her middle finger, as she headed out the door. Jason stood there baffled, and oddly aroused all at the same time. *What the fuck just happened?*

9

Try the Crema Segrato

Earlier that same evening, before Jason and Matt had to save Tommy from an epic beating at the hands of Crazy Mike. JP and Mandy met up at a fancy new restaurant in Tribeca to discuss how Mandy would sub in for JP, while he was on sabbatical to his home in South Africa. Upon arriving they were greeted by the Maître D', a slight woman with her hair slicked back. She was short, thin, and completely nude.

"Good evening, and welcome to Teatro dei Vegenitali." She said.

Mandy gasped softly, making sure that she was seeing what she thought she was. *Oh my god, where am I?*

"Good evening," JP said as if this was all perfectly normal. "We have an 8 o'clock reservation for two, under John Paul."

"Ah yes, Mister Paul. You're Chef Rocco's special guest. Welcome, welcome. Please, follow me. Your table is waiting."

The Maître D' stepped out from behind the standing desk and walked ahead of them toward the main dining room. JP stepped out of the way, kindly gesturing at Mandy that she should walk ahead.

The restaurant was packed with patrons. Nude wait staff bustled around the room, taking orders, tending to their assigned tables. It was almost elegant but Mandy found it to be a little too much to be casual about.

"So, um, how did you find out about this place?" Mandy asked as they walked through the room dodging naked servers, who weaved to and fro among the patrons.

"I know, it's so new age right?" JP said excitedly as they arrived at their table. The Maître D' pulled out Mandy's chair, exposing her rear to the entire room. JP waited for Mandy to sit. "My client is the chef here, Rocco Giovanni. Have you heard of him?"

Mandy sat down, trying to avoid contact with the Maître D as she shoved her chair in. "No, I can't say that I have." She said, unable to recall the chef's name.

JP sat down and unfolded his napkin, placing it on his lap. "Well, he has a cooking show on the Eats Network called Vegging Out; it's mediocre at best, but it pays for his sessions, I suppose. He seems to think he's God's gift to vegetarian cuisine." Mandy rolled her eyes. "But despite all that, I hear the food here is to die for. Each and every plate is a work of art."

"Wow, that's interesting," Mandy said. "I hope it tastes as good as it looks."

She wondered why JP would bring her to such a place for a business meeting.

JP leaned over the table and looked Mandy square in the eyes. "Mandy, I'm so happy you agreed to take over my classes while I'm away. I really don't know if I could've trusted anyone else."

"Aww. Thank you JP. I'm glad you have so much confidence in me."

"The thought of having some new Yoga Werx wannabe instructor leading my students is dreadful. I thank God everyday I have you."

"Stop JP, I'm blushing." Mandy said, jokingly.

JP put his hand on Mandy's. "No really. I thank Him everyday."

Mandy laughed. JP continued looking straight into her eyes intensely, seemingly confused at what she found so funny. Slowly Mandy realized that JP wasn't kidding. She started to draw her hand back. *What's going on here?*

Their waiter, who, also completely nude approached the table with two menus, mercifully interrupted the awkward silence. "Hello my name is Rory and I will be your server for the evening."

Mandy, too embarrassed to look the waiter in the eye, tried to cover the side of her face with her hand.

The waiter continued, un-phased. "Would you like to have today's specials? Chef Rocco has definitely outdone himself this time." He handed them their menus.

JP nodded his head. "Yes please, I would love that."

Mandy quickly covered her face with the menu, pretending not to notice the waiter's penis dangling over their table.

"Tonight, we have the Grilled Organic Pene Melanzana Ensalata. The eggplant is lightly seared to perfection, basted and injected with Chef Rocco's crema segreto, placed on a bed of crisp, locally grown mixed vegetables. We also have a gluten-free, dairy-free, organic, hemp cunnilinguini alfredo—again topped with the Chef's crema segreto—served with two tofu polpettes on the side." Mandy squirmed in her chair as the naked server continued. JP looked him straight in the face, beaming.

"Finally, we have the soups of day. First, we have the Tofu Testicoli Zuppa al Pesto and finally, we have Chef Rocco's Rich Crema Segreto Zuppa."

"You know, what they need more of?" JP said jokingly, opening his menu. "Some of that Crema Segreto."

"Oh no," The waiter replied, unaware that he was being mocked. "Chef Rocco insists on making just one batch of his famous crema segreto every day. It is fresh every morning."

"Really, just one batch?" JP said, looking to see if Mandy caught the joke. She was looking intently at the ceiling, waiting for the naked waiter to finish.

"Please take your time, look at the menu and I'll be back. Can I get anyone something to drink?"

"A bottle of the house cabernet should be just fine," JP said.

"I'm going to stick with sparkling water," Mandy added. "I have early morning class tomorrow."

"Oh come now, not even one drink?" JP asked.

"No, but thank you." Mandy said, trying to keep things as professional as possible given the absurd circumstances. "I have to be up early. My brain is on business mode and my fiancé is annoyed with me because I ditched him last minute to come here. So I'd rather really not drink. I think it would just make things worse."

JP looked slightly taken aback. "Goodness dear, I apologize for my insensitive behavior. I had no idea." Mandy breathed a sigh of relief. She felt the pressure easing as she took a sip of her water. JP continued. "I totally understand how you feel. Stress does terrible things to the body. Let's focus on why we're here."

Mandy caught a glimpse of something out of the corner of her eye. She turned around to see what it was and all of a sudden found herself about 4 inches away from the waiter's dangling penis. She jumped back startled. *Jesus, what the fuck?*

The waiter poured a glass of sparking water for Mandy. "Sparkling water for Madame." He walked around the table and started uncorking a bottle of wine. "And cabernet for Signore." He poured a sip for JP to taste. JP gulped it down and nodded approvingly. The waiter started pouring a full glass. "Do you need more time with the menu?"

JP Turned to Mandy. "I'm not sure, are you ready to order?" he asked.

"No, go ahead, I'm still looking." She said, turning to the next page on the menu.

JP looked up at the waiter. "Well then, I'll have the eggplant salad."

"You know what, I'll just take the tossed salad." Mandy said.

The waiter wrote down their orders on a penis-shaped notepad. "One Grilled Organic Pene Melanzana Ensalata and one tossed ensalata. Extra primo. Coming right up." He stepped back, turned, and walked away leaving JP and Mandy in an awkward silence. JP picked up his wine glass and swirled it a bit. Sensing Mandy's malaise, he held up his glass. "Cheers! To you, darling."

"Cheers," Mandy answered, half-heartedly. She raised her sparkling water. They clinked their glasses together.

"So, what did you have in mind in terms of classes and scheduling?" Mandy asked.

JP brushed aside her question. "I'll email you the details, darling. Please apologize to your fiancé for me. I should never have insisted on meeting with you tonight."

Mandy immediately saw through JP's insincere attempt to disarm the situation but she decided to play along anyway, at least for long enough to find out what the job entailed. "I'll be sure to let him know." She said. "So, what are you doing on your hiatus? Let's talk about your trip since all the teaching logistics will be covered over email."

"I'm flying home to South Africa. I haven't been there since I was a boy." JP Said.

"That's great! Are you going to see your family?"

"Not really, my mother and father were killed trying to calm tensions between students and police during the Soweto uprising in the seventies." JP said, solemnly. "Our housekeeper adopted me and raised me, along with her daughter until I was old enough to take care of myself."

"Oh… I'm so sorry. I must've sounded like an idiot just now." Mandy said, embarrassed.

"Nonsense! It was long ago. I was just a boy," JP reassured her. "Besides, it'll be nice to get out of the city, away from the gym and away from some of these people."

"What do you mean?"

"You know, these God awful people at the gym: the fakes, the pretenders, those who make a living by pulling the wool over people's eyes." JP sipped his wine.

"Who are you, J.P. Salinger? What do you mean fakes and pretenders?"

"Oh please darling, don't tell me you've fallen for it. *'Ra! Ra! We are the best gym in the world.* What nonsense." JP scoffed.

"Why not? I love it there. Everybody's so friendly."

"Mandy, please. You must understand the situation. The Grand is a house of cards, set to collapse. I don't even know how it's managed to stay afloat this long."

"But Vanessa said, membership is up and that—"

"That's because she waved the $1000 initial fee in order to sell more memberships. Christ, Mandy, you must be more informed. The economy has been in the shitter for so long, nobody was going to pay those prices, especially when they can get a better deal elsewhere. The Grand can barely cover their expenses. Vanessa is just delaying the inevitable. The sooner Fit Corp takes over, the better it will be for everyone. Better management, better margins, a more refined and illustrious clientele, and no more hooligan trainers. I can barely wait, can't you?" JP said, twirling his glass of wine.

Mandy found herself thinking of Jason and his dumb ass friends.

She was still doubtful of JP's claim. "Don't you think somebody would've caught on by now though? I mean someone needs to approve this right? She just can't go and change things around on a whim like that."

"Well, Mandy—and this is strictly between you and me—from I what hear, somebody has caught on. They're not saying anything yet. I think they want see Vanessa publicly disgraced. It's all so diabolical." He shook his head. "It's quite sad really, so base, so pitiable. That's why she's been on the warpath with the personal training department—to bring in more money. If you ask me, I think she should just fire all them, starting with that fat one, Jason."

Mandy looked at JP crossly. "Why Jason? He's the busiest trainer at the gym."

JP scoffed. "Brutish, unrefined, immature, manner-less and out of shape. He's a hack. I'm not sure he's even qualified to change the towels."

"He's not out of shape," Mandy objected. "He just needs to tweak a few things with his diet." Mandy became increasingly defensive. "Plus he's very knowledgeable about fitness, he genuinely cares for people, and he gets results for his clients. Isn't that what really matters? Fit Corp would just raise prices and lower wages for its employees, where's the good in that?"

JP, taken a little off guard by Mandy's defensiveness, paused for a moment before responding quietly. "I wonder if somebody's fiancé would be concerned over his girlfriend's fondness for a colleague?" He said, pouring another glass of wine. "Does he know about your little work crush?"

"That is really uncalled for!" Mandy said, exasperated. "I would have you know—" She stopped mid-sentence, spotting something from the corner of her eye.

"Oh look, just in time! I do believe I'm famished." JP said as the waiter brought the food to the table.

Mandy was aghast by the array. What she thought was supposed to be a regular tossed salad looked more like an edible buttocks made from two cantaloupe halves, scooped out and garnished with a half a cherry making it look like an anus on a bed of fruit and vegetables She looked over at JP's plate a large Phallic eggplant over a bed mixed greens with two walnuts placed at one end, resembling testicles. *Oh. My God!*

"One Grilled Organic Pene Melanzana Ensalata. Enjoy!" said the waiter, stepping back, slightly bowing, and leaving the table once again.

JP picked up a small spoon, dipped it into the crema segrato, and then drizzled the sauce over his dish. "Bon appetite," he said, slicing into the tip of the eggplant, putting it into his mouth and masticating it, as if it were foreplay. "Mm, Yeah. The flavor really explodes in my mouth," he continued, smiling at Mandy, who was at this point completely flabbergasted. "Would you like to try it?"

"No thank you, I have more than enough on my plate," she replied, picking at her salad, not really sure where to start.

"So as I was saying, those idiots aren't going to last long," JP said, with his mouth full.

"Really, how so?"

JP took another bite of his eggplant, this time barely chewing. "Well, as you know, us yogis get paid for the classes we teach, so it doesn't matter how many people we have in the class—either way the pay is same. The trainers, though, they get paid for the amount of people they train. If they're not getting new clients or getting their existing clients to buy more sessions, nobody's making any money. That negatively impacts the gym's profit margin and Vanessa truly *hates* that." JP cracked open a walnut, and popped it in his mouth.

"So if the trainers don't make their quota, they get fired?" Mandy asked.

JP finished his second glass of wine. "Precisely. As I understand it, they have ninety days to bring their numbers up, or they get…" JP took a knife and waved it across his throat. "But from what I'm hearing, the Grand's Board of Directors is going to fire Vanessa either way."

"How do you know that?" Mandy asked.

JP poured himself a third full glass of wine. "One of my students is fucking someone on the board."

"And she told you all this?"

"*He* told me all this."

"The board members are all men though, I didn't realize any of them were gay"

"Evidently one is," JP Said. "He's also married, with grandchildren."

"What!?" Mandy exclaimed.

"Oh, you have no idea what's going on do you?"

Mandy had barely touched her food. The sheer volume of new information had finished off whatever appetite she may have had after the initial shock of dangling penises and exposed asses wore off.

"So let me get this straight, the trainers have to sell more personal training in order to keep their jobs so that Vanessa can show that the gym's still making money. But even if they do that and she can, she's still gonna lose her job?"

"Intriguing, isn't it?" JP said, grinning smugly. He took another huge sip of wine. "I can't wait to see how this all turns out, should be quite a show."

Mandy's stomach began to turn from JP's gauche excitement but she maintained her composure. She tried to force herself to eat her salad, careful to not tip him off about her uneasiness. *Quite a show indeed...What a scumbag.*

Suddenly a voice boomed out from the direction of the kitchen. "JP! Is that you man!?" It was Chef Rocco, a tall and rotund man wearing nothing but a stained apron, a toque, and orange crocs with black knee-high socks. He jaunted over to their table, wiping his hands in his apron.

"Wow, even in the kitchen." Mandy said, looking Rocco up and down.

JP opened his arm to receive a hug from Rocco.

"It's great to see you JP, how are you?"

"My God Rocco! Do you have to try everything before you serve it, how much weight have you gained?"

Rocco laughed cavernously. "You've never been a subtle man. Twenty five pounds."

"My lord," said JP.

"It's been nonstop for me since my show, now this restaurant. I haven't worked out in weeks, but that'll change once we hire more people." Rocco looked over at Mandy.

"This is Amanda, she's a colleague. We've been discussing some business over dinner, which by the way is extraordinary." JP gulped down his third glass of wine and rubbed his stomach dramatically.

"Why thank you—so nice to meet you Amanda. I see you got the organic tossed ensalata, one of my favorites. It comes with jelly or syrup. I prefer the syrup myself."

"Nice to meet you too Chef. I'll make sure to try both." Mandy said hesitantly.

JP leaned over and prodded Rocco in the stomach. "And when was the last time you ate salad, let alone tossed one?"

"JP!" Mandy interjected. "That's rude!"

Rocco smiled at Mandy. "I expect no less from Jean-Paul. Kindness is a sign of weakness for him. Didn't you know that already?" He and JP started cracking up.

"You know I'm just busting your chops. Mandy's going to think I'm sort of a monster." JP said, staring at Mandy. "And I'm sure her fiancé wouldn't approve of her cavorting with such people."

"My fiancé also appreciates that I can handle myself." Mandy said coolly.

Rocco laughed again. "There you go, JP. can't go five minutes without being an asshole."

JP started pouring himself another glass. "I blame the wine. It has an effect on me. I think I'll have another glass." He said dismissively. Rocco shook his head as JP emptied the bottle in his glass.

Suddenly, a naked bus boy rushed over to the Chef and whispered something in his ear. "Oh my, sorry to cut this short," Rocco said, "but I'm afraid I have to get back to the kitchen. There's an issue that needs my prompt attention." He backed away from the table and turned around, exposing his hairy backside to Mandy. She heaved a little bit but stopped herself from actually vomiting.

JP continued drinking his wine aggressively. "Huh. Well that was a pleasure. The chef himself came out to greet us." Mandy stared at her half-eaten salad. "Don't you think so Mandy?"

"It was something alright." She said, taking a sip of water. "You know it's getting late…"

"Don't tell me you have to go. You've barely touched your food!"

"Honestly, I have four back to back classes tomorrow starting at 6am, so I'd better be going."

JP finished his wine. "I understand. It's just that, well, I thought we shared a special connection Mandy."

"A…special connection?" she asked skeptically.

JP picked up the empty wine bottle to see if anything was left. He turned it upside down and tried to catch the last few drops on his tongue, missing and dripping them on his shirt. "Yeah, I was thinking that we would have dinner and then go over to my place to discuss business, maybe have a digestive, perhaps even order some desert for after—er, later."

"I'm sorry," Mandy said irately, "but I was under the impression that this was a business meeting, not some pathetic attempt to get me into bed."

"I thought you wanted to take over the empire," JP slurred, somewhat desperately, "to teach the masses, inspire people who will adore you, follow you… fall in love with you. And in the meantime you'd be making more money than you ever have practicing yoga. I can see now that you weren't serious in your commitment to this life. It's really quite disappointing Mandy, I thought you were special. You should be flattered I would even think of you. I mean, you're hot and all, but I'm. Well…"

Mandy stood up abruptly. "Look JP, I'm not going to cheat on Steve to grow my business, least of all with you. Do you really think so little of me, that this stunt would work?" JP glared at her with contempt. Mandy took out a handful of cash and threw it on the table. "You are a sad little man. I gotta go."

Mandy threw on her coat and walked toward the exit, bumping into a naked server on her way out and causing him to fall penis-first into a nearby customer's soup causing a scene as she stormed out the door. JP signaled to the waiter for more wine, picked up his knife and fork, and resumed eating his meal. All of a sudden he made a sour face and stopped chewing. He reached into his mouth and pulled out a short curly hair. *Ugh!*

10

Rise and Grind

It was 4:45 am and Jason was just getting home. He staggered into his cramped studio apartment, scuffing the floor with every uneven step. He was barely able to walk straight. He managed to kick off one shoe but had trouble getting the other one off. He leaned into the wall and pulled the shoe off with his hands. He unbuttoned his pants and ripped one leg off, falling onto the floor. He furiously kicked at the other leg, trying to get it to come off his ankle. Finally he peeled it off and stood back up. Lurching and leering, he stumbled toward the bathroom, swaying side to side, reaching out for anything that might hold him up. He turned on the light and began to urinate, first into the toilet, then onto the seat and then onto the floor. He let go of a big yawn and an even bigger fart.

"What'd you say asshole?" He laughed to himself.

He walked over his futon, stepping on a pizza box from Luigi's along the way and getting cheesy grease on his feet from the leftover slice inside. He shoved all the clothes on his futon onto the floor in a heap. He tried to lie down carefully so as not to aggravate his throbbing headache or worse, give himself the spins, but he was unable to control his movement and he slipped, rolling right off the futon and tumbling face first into his pile of dirty clothes.

Somehow he managed to roll over, his blood shot eyes stared up at the ceiling. It began to spin and wobble. *Please God, don't let me throw up.* His eyelids started to feel extra heavy, and slowly the drooped down, covering everything in darkness, a sure sign that he would soon be dozing off. *Oh thank you, thank you, thank you.*

Aangh! Aangh! Aangh! All of a sudden, a brutal, high pitched sound rung out, snapping Jason out of his tranquility. The alarm on his phone had gone off. The noise traveled through the air, piercing Jason's eardrums, like invisible daggers. Bringing his headache back with a vengeance. He sat up, lunged for his phone, but instead knocked over the bedside table, along with a bottle of skin lotion, an ashtray filled with marijuana ashes, a table lamp, and his phone still blaring.

"Ugh..." His bloodshot eyes peeled open as his brain came back online. Pawing at the floor, until he got a hold of his phone. The time: 5:15 am. He rolled back over to snooze, but a feeling began to wash over him, something was missing? Then, it dawned on him. The alarm was set to remind him that he had a 6:00 am client. *Fuuuuck me!*

Later that same morning, Lois Hirsch, a portly, middle-aged woman; with thick glasses, and a snarky demeanor, approached the receptionist at the fitness desk. "Excuse me *Sheila*, but have you seen Matt? We were supposed to train at 6:00."

"Good morning Mrs. Hirsch!" Sheila replied. "Of course, let me help you with that!" Sheila cracked a warm, plastic smile, as she looked for his number in the employee directory.

"I'm sure he's around here somewhere, Mrs. Hirsch, it's not like Matt to be late for an appointment. He lives for his clients!" Lois feigned a smile and looked at her watch. 6:25 am.

"Oh! Here comes someone that might know!" Sheila said cheerfully as she pointed to Jason, who was just walking in, looking pale as death. He had a half eaten banana in one hand and a large coffee in the other.

"Excuse me, Jay!" Jay looked at her with a death stare. *Do not even fuck with me right now, Sheila, you cheery bitch.* "Hi um, do you know if Matt's in today?" She asked. "His 6:00 o'clock client is here looking for him!"

Jason paused for a second, took a deep breath and sighed. He walked over to the desk. His eyebrows furrowed as he attempts to concentrate through the throbbing pain in his head, wincing from the bright lights of the gym. His mind ran through a hazy montage of events from the night before. He was putting things together in his head like a puzzle with missing pieces, except that it felt like someone is a jamming a corkscrew into his temples at the same time.

He remembered being on stage, bringing up Crazy Mike, and

running out of the club to catch up with Matt and Tommy. A little while later, he wasn't sure when, they were at a bar throwing back copious amounts of tequila. He remembered at one point Matt getting punched in the face after groping a woman that Jason had convinced him was a man. Then it was blank. His mind flashed forward. The guys were pissing outside. Out of nowhere a police siren goes off, causing them to scatter midstream, piss all over themselves and each other. Finally, he remembered Matt deciding to get into a three-point football stance, call out a play, say hike, and try to sack a tree head on, then waking up as he was being placed in the back of an ambulance, only to leap off the gurney and dart off into the night.

Jason was convinced that Matt was either in jail, blacked out on a subway, or curled up in the corner of some after hours club that was still open. Either way he would definitely not be in. He turned to Mrs. Hirsch. "Uh. I'm not so sure Matt is going to—"

"Hey! Good morning everybody!" Matt strolled in nonchalantly. "Lois, I am so sorry about my tardiness! Trains were crazy. I promise I'll make it up to you!" He looked totally fine. In fact, he looked like he hadn't even been out the night before.

"…Make you wait much longer?" Jason said baffled, as he tried to amend his sentence.

"Don't worry Lois, I'm going to give you an extra special stretching session today. How 'bout that!?" Matt said, giving her a gentle pat on the back. She looked absolutely giddy.

Matt walked over to Jason, patted him on the shoulders, fixed his shirt and adjusted his nametag. "Hey buddy, you alright? You don't look so good. Better finish that coffee. It's a brand new day!"

Matt walked off with Mrs. Hirsch to their session. Jason stood there with his mouth agape, utterly stupefied. There was literally no way Matt could have been okay after what happened the night before. *What?*

11

Slag Bitches Took My Room

"Congratulations on your new promotion." Said Carla. "You've come a long way in a short period of time. You should be proud."

"I am… Thank you so much, this means a lot." Said Barbara.

Carla Simpson was The Grand's General Manager. She oversaw the gym's entire operations; from daily meetings with department supervisors and unannounced white glove inspections, to quarterly profit/loss report meetings with corporate, and several other important duties required to operate the largest, most luxurious fitness facility in the entire world. Carla was a well-liked and highly regarded General Manager. With an MBA from NYU, She ran The Grand like a well-oiled machine. Most employees adored her. Those that didn't respected her.

On this day, she was in the spa promoting Barbara Stewart, a massage therapist at The Grand to the Spa Supervisor position.

"You won't be disappointed Carla, I'm going to turn this place into a destination," Barbara said, enthusiastically "I have so many ideas that I want to implement. 2008 will be our best year ever, you'll see."

"I can't wait… I know you'll do an outstanding job."

Carla began to press on her own shoulder, wincing at some discomfort she'd been having. "Not to rain on your parade, but my shoulder's been bugging me again."

"You should really book an appointment." Barbara said, "Let's do that while we're here."

"Ugh… I really don't have time my schedule is too hectic. What about right now? I could really use a deep-tissue massage. My back's also been bothering me and I only have thirty minutes before my next meeting." Carla said, stretching her back.

"Well we really don't have any available rooms at this moment," Barbara said, walking behind the receptionist's desk. Let's see… it's now 12:20, there's one room available until 12:30. That's not enough time. Let's make it for later this evening, it'll be slower then."

"Are you sure Barb? I could really use your help now actually."

"I really can't, it's cutting it too close."

Carla gave Barbara a glance that made her nervous.

"Um… I don't think it's a good idea, but… how can I refuse the boss, right?"

"Oh thank you Barbara, I really need those magic hands of yours. You have no idea what my life is like."

"Then pleasure is all mine, I guess."

Barbara hesitantly leads Carla back toward the treatment rooms.

Not a minute later, Vanessa arrives for her 12:30 client, who would be arriving any second. She put on her uniform and walked over to the supply closet to get the customary plush white robe and flip-flops that clients received upon entering the spa. She heard door to the spa swing open. *There he is, right on time.*

"I'll be right with you Henry," Vanessa said, calling out from the supply closet. "I left you the robe. Go ahead and change, while I get the room ready."

Vanessa made her way down the dimly lit hallway looking for a room.

The doors all had little the red and gold tassels on the knob, indicating that the rooms were all being occupied. *That's strange, why aren't there any rooms available?*

Henry walked out of the changing room, ready to be worked on.

"How are you doing today?" Henry asked.

"I'm splendid Henry. However, there seems to be a little mix up here." She said, looking through the schedule. "I have you down for 12:30, but there doesn't seem to be a room available. Would you mind waiting for just one moment? "

"Sure." Henry said.

Vanessa put her ear to each door, listening for any recognizable voices. But, there was very little talking. She went back to Henry, who was still sitting in the waiting area, flipping through sports magazine.

"I'm sorry Henry, but there don't seem to be any rooms available, and the next one doesn't open up until 1:00 pm." She explained, "I don't know what happened, I booked this appointment myself."

"Well that's disappointing. Clearly if the appointment is there, then there should be a room available." He said.

"That's correct…"

"Then why isn't there a room? I'm here on my lunch break to see you and now you're telling me that there is no room available, even though you put it on the schedule." Henry said, turning a bit pink in the face.

"I'm sorry Mr. Fields. I will get to the bottom of this, right away. In the meantime can you wait for the next room?"

"No, Vanessa I can't. This is completely unprofessional. I expect a certain level a service when I come here. That's why I pay these outrageously high membership fees. So when something goes wrong, you can understand my frustrations."

Vanessa stammered to find the right words. "Certainly, but, but…"

"I'm leaving now. I will also be calling the management later to let them know about this debacle." He said.

"Yes of course…" Vanessa said weakly.

Henry changed back into his business attire, and stormed out in a huff. Leaving Vanessa standing there humiliated. Puzzled, she sat down on the couch, trying to figure out how she could've messed up. *I've been doing this too long, something's not right.*

She got up from the couch and went back to the room she reserved. Carefully, she put her ear to the door, listening for any sounds, while turning the knob.

Vanessa barley cracked the door open, when she saw what looked like the silhouette of two women performing oral sex on each other. Quickly, but quietly she closed the door, stunned by what she saw. *Slag bitches took my room.*

Moments later, Carla followed by Barbara came out from one of the rooms. Vanessa was behind the reception desk, pretending to be on the computer.

"Thank you so much for fitting me in, you're a real godsend." Carla said, giddily walking past Vanessa. "Oh, hi Vanessa, didn't know you were here. How are you today?"

Vanessa stood there glaring at Barbara but she looks away sheepishly.

"Are you okay?" Carla asked.

"I'm having a bit of a rough day, but nothing that I can't—" Vanessa said, turning to Carla.

"Oops look at the time!" Carla interrupted. "Let's chat over some tea sometime. I want to get to know the highest earning masseuse at The Grand better. I really must get going."

"That would be nice." She said, tensing her jaw.

"Oh, and before I forget, say hi to your new supervisor. I just promoted Barbara today." Carla said, walking toward the door, "Toodles everybody."

Carla opened the door and walked out. Vanessa turned toward Barbara.

"Supervisor eh…"

"I know I messed up, I told her we had fifteen minutes," Barbara said. "She kept asking for two more minutes, but two minutes turned into twenty."

"…Turned into twenty." Repeated Vanessa.

"You know what a scatter brain, she is."

Vanessa stood there silent.

"Say something. You're making me uncomfortable… Vanessa!"

"I booked an appointment for 12:30 pm, two weeks ago." Vanessa said, furiously, "You threw me under the bus. I lost money today and you made me look bad! I have to say Barbara that was really unprofessional and I'm really disappointed. But maybe, that's the kind of thing I should expect from someone with less experience and less time working here."

"I don't appreciate the insubordinate tone." Barbara said, pulling rank, reminding Vanessa of her new authority. "Let's call your client and we'll give him a massage session on us. I'll also keep you booked solid for the next month. How does that sound?"

Nothing but silence from Vanessa.

"In the meantime, I need the rooms re-stocked. We don't have a receptionist today, so you're going to have to do it."

"Whatever you say boss…" Vanessa said, walking back toward the supply room, "You know I was going to invite you out to lunch to celebrate your promotion. But, I see you've already *eaten* your fill."

Barbara gasps softly as she watches Vanessa leave.

12

'Roids all the Rage

Jennifer tidied up her desk, answered a few phone calls and gathered everything she needed in preparation for Vanessa's meeting with The Grand's Board of Directors. She waited patiently at Vanessa's office door with her chin up and shoulders back like a soldier standing at attention. She was eager to impress her captain with her thoroughness. She pulled out her tablet to go through the day's schedule one more time and make sure she hadn't missed any details. *The car is waiting. Check. P and L files in the bag. Check. Vanessa's dry cleaning sent out. Check.*

Minutes went by and Vanessa still hadn't come out of her office. Jennifer looked at her watch to check the time. She put the tablet in camera mode to check her hair, make-up, and teeth. Fifteen more minutes passed, and still not a word from Vanessa. Jennifer's feet were getting tired She took off a shoe to rub her foot. Unsure about what was going on with Vanessa, Jennifer began to feel fatigued from standing there for so long. She walked back to her desk to sit down, but before her butt could touch the chair, Vanessa burst out of her office.

"No time to dilly dally, Miss Diego!" Vanessa said. "This meeting is of the upmost importance."

Here we go. Jennifer sighed, trying to catch up to Vanessa, one shoe half on as she hobbled into the elevator.

A car service took them midtown, to the offices of Chilmark Holdings, The Grand's parent company. Vanessa reviewed the documents on their way to the meeting, preparing herself for the presentation. "Everything seems to be in order," said Vanessa, handing the documents back to Jennifer.

"I tripled checked everything to make sure!" Said Jennifer, hoping to get some recognition for her work.

"As you should have!" Said Vanessa, looking out the window.

The black sedan pulled up to the building. The driver got out, walked around to the back, and opened the door. Vanessa stepped out first, "Thank you." She said.

Jennifer struggled to climb out of the car because of the all stuff she was carrying. The driver held her bag while she stood up and adjusted her dress.

"Thank you, very much." She said, taking her things back, walking hurriedly behind Vanessa who was already ten paces ahead. Jennifer felt the faint buzz of her phone vibrating. She reached into her bag and took it out. It was an email. Jennifer's olive skin went pale as she read it. A look of terror came over her face. *Aye Dios Mio… This is bad.* She ran up to Vanessa in a panic.

"Vanessa wait, you have to read this." She said, trying to catch her breath.

"Come on then, what is it? We don't have all day." Vanessa said, impatiently.

Unable to talk from sprinting, Jennifer managed to blurt out "just read" as she handed her phone to Vanessa.

Vanessa read through the email. *Bollocks!* It was a headline from the Post: ***Roids All The Rage At Mega Gym.***

"This article is going to be on Page Six tomorrow." Said Vanessa, taking a deep breath.

"Maybe no one will care," Jennifer said. "The New York Post is more tabloid fodder than real journalism anyway, right?"

"What in bloody hell is going on?" Vanessa thought out loud. "Call them back, right now and tell them if they run that story, I will sue."

She handed the phone back and Jennifer began to dial. They walked past the reception desk.

"Excuse me, do you have an appointment?" asked the receptionist.

Vanessa passed by, barely acknowledging her presence. Jennifer followed her closely, with her phone in one ear.

"Oh, hi, sorry about that!" Jennifer said, apologizing for Vanessa's discourteousness. "We're here for an 11:00 o'clock appointment with the board. Vanessa—Hi yes, hello." She said, gesturing to the phone.

"11:00 o'clock, ok here we are…" Said the receptionist. "They're waiting for you in the conference room."

Preoccupied with the phone, Jennifer gave the receptionist one thumbs up and rushed back to Vanessa. "I need to speak with someone regarding tomorrow's story on Page Six. Yes I'll hold." She said, switching ears.

Vanessa was silent. Her eyes focused straight ahead as the elevator went up to the penthouse offices. The doors slid open. They both stepped out and walked down a starkly lit hallway with rows of black and white photographs of city landmarks on both sides. At the other end of the hallway there was a pair of large mahogany doors, light from the other side gleamed through; creating an aura around the doors that was quite intimidating.

Vanessa opened the doors and walked into a large room with dark wood paneling on one side and large windows on the other. Through them was a view of the Empire State Building. In the middle of the room were three men in suits, seated around a large oblong table, chattering quietly. All the way at the end of the room was a slide projector pointed at a screen. On the screen, plain as day, was the page six headline *"Roids All The Rage, At Mega-Gym."* The men stopped what they were doing and looked in Vanessa's direction.

Vanessa took a deep breath. "Good morning gentlemen, I see I don't have to bring you up to speed on these libelous accusations." She took a seat at the other end of the table. Jennifer laid out Vanessa's things on the table and walked back by the doors, waiting for someone to get back to her on the phone.

"Good morning ladies, I hope you find yourselves well," said Stuart Holman, CEO of Chilmark Holdings. Stuart was a tall slender man with salt and pepper hair, a square jaw and icy blue eyes. His skin was tan and weathered from years of competing in triathlons and laying out on beaches without sunscreen.

Vanessa nodded her head politely. "I was unaware that we'd be amending the itinerary for this morning, I would've come even more prepared to—"

"Of course you are" Interrupted Thomas Richards, who was sitting next to Stuart. "I trust that addressing this urgent situation first won't be a problem."

"No problem at all, Mr. Richards." Vanessa gulped, turning her eyes away from him. "Let's get to it then, Mr. Holman, please continue."

Mr. Holman looked up from his documents at Vanessa. "Mr. Richards is right not to put it mildly, Vanessa. Let's not beat around the bush here. I hope you realize the seriousness of these allegations."

His demeanor was calm, but the concern in his voice was unmistakable. "Something like this could ruin our reputation and hurt our business. It could even leave us vulnerable to takeover."

"Yes, of course." Vanessa agreed. "It is serious indeed, which is why I have personally taken it upon myself to get to the bottom of this." Vanessa looked around the room at the board members. "Of course, you'll understand, I will need time, resources, and—"

"Time! Resources!" Interrupted Mr. Richards again. "Ms. Todd, don't you think a lengthy investigation at this juncture, is a bit too late. You are aware the story comes out tomorrow."

"If it's the timing of the story you're concerned with, then perhaps Mr. Richards, we should start with who could have leaked this story in the first place." Vanessa replied, glaring at him. "After all, we don't want to spook our investors. It's been hard enough keeping them on board since the crash in '08.

I am well aware of what a scandal like this could do to our share prices and with the investor meeting only two days away. If we don't stop this story now, and find out who was behind it, then we may as well scrap today's itinerary as well because we'll all be watching our stock prices drop like stones and looking for new jobs. I suggest we get in front of it now, while we still can."

Mr. Richards was visibly frustrated that Vanessa had not immediately accepted responsibility. However, before he could speak, Jacob Feinberg cleared his throat demonstratively. He was a small man, about five and a half feet tall. He wore thin-framed glasses and a yamaka covering his balding head. He sat directly across Thomas.

"If I may interject, Thomas, Ms. Todd has a point. Whoever

leaked this story may be trying to sabotage the investor meeting in order to create an environment of fear and disorder. One in which Fit Corp would be perfectly positioned to come in and snatch us up."

Mr. Richards dismissed what Jacob had just said. "All drama aside for a moment, the fact of the matter is: we are going to have a public relations nightmare on our hands tomorrow if we don't do something about it today. Now, I don't see any evidence of any corporate sabotage. All I see is a great company being run into the ground because of poor and inexperienced management. I propose we bear down and weather this storm: replace all management from the Grand with a staff of experienced professionals who can better avoid future catastrophes."

Vanessa sat up tall, crossing her hands. "Very well, Mr. Richards. If you all genuinely believe that I am to blame for this bungle, then I expect you to have sufficient evidence to that fact." She looked at Thomas. "Go on then, where is it?"

Mr. Richards was incensed. "This is the unprofessional, insubordinate behavior I'm talking about! What makes you think you have authority here? You don't get to question me!" He said disdainfully.

"I beg your pardon, Mr. Richards, but when my integrity and abilities are brought into question without sufficient cause, am I supposed to sit idly by while you deliberate my future at this company without defending myself? I'm sorry gentlemen, but even us English have a limit to our sense of proper decorum."

The men in the room were surprised by Vanessa's tone.

She continued. "How is it, that all of the sudden, everything that I've accomplished for this company has been disregarded, as if my actions didn't keep our doors open through a recession and an investor scare unlike anything this company has faced before? Has everyone forgotten, that during my four-year tenure, as General Manager; we have managed to reorganize how we do, business. We were able to adapt to this new economy and manage to remain open. All while our competitors, have gone out of business.

I don't know if you've had a chance to walk around the city lately, but there are a lot of places *still* going out of business. Have you seen the empty storefronts? My god, 1st avenue is a ghost town from here to 86th street. The middle class are leaving in droves. They can't afford to live here anymore, and they certainly can't afford high-end gym memberships. The only people who will be left before long will be the rich and famous, and poor and hungry. How long before it all goes to shite, then? Only one of those groups can afford a membership to the Grand. The good news is that we're still here, the worst is over, here's my proof."

Vanessa pulled out folders containing The Grand's profit and loss statements from the previous three months. She leaned in and slid the folders to everyone. "With an average of ten percent increases in membership for each of the past eight months, revenue has increased *exponentially*, which has legitimately brought us out of the red, staying a hostile takeover by Fit Corp. All of the numbers are right here to prove it. This is what our shareholders want to hear. Properly informed, they won't mind a single allegation of impropriety. Especially, from the *Post* of all places."

Mr. Holman stared at his folder, without opening it. He sighed. "Ms. Todd, I'm going to be frank with you. The purpose of this meeting was to ask for your resignation."

Jacob took the folder and opened it. Mr. Holman continued. "This is not the first time the Grand has had bad publicity." Mr. Holman picked up the clicker for the projector. He pulled up an image of the New York Post headline: **Sleeping Woman Flies Car Into Hudson.** Underneath it was an image of a car being pulled out of the Hudson River, and a mugshot of Carla Simpson's bruised face in the lower right corner.

"Four years ago, Carla Simpson, your predecessor, overdosed on muscle relaxers and drove her car into the Hudson. She almost died."

"Of course, that was tragic." Replied Vanessa, "When is her next court hearing, by the way?"

"Not for another two months." Mr. Holman continued. "The strangest part of that whole incident was that they never found a medicine bottle, nor did she have a prescription for muscle relaxers. Yet somehow, copious amounts of it, was found in her system."

Vanessa responded, "These days, people can get any drug they want, for the right price. I respected Carla, but that woman was a fiend, I caught her having sex with an employee in one of the massage rooms. In any case, I fail to see what her actions have to do with my performance."

"Yes, I suppose, that is that case." Said Mr. Holman.

He clicked the remote again, pulling up a video clip of JP on NBC's Today Show, demonstrating some yoga poses to Katy Beth and Maya. As JP, showed them tree pose, Katy Beth, loses her balance and falls into JP; who then knocks, Maya into the Camera.

JP gets up angrily, "You fokken, lush!"

Everyone gasps in shock, as the camera cuts to a "technical difficulties" color block.

Mr. Holman paused the video clip. "Then one of your employees called Maya Reynolds, America's sweetheart, a drunk on national television!"

Jennifer walked up to Vanessa, leaned down, and whispered, "The Post is not going to pull the story."

"Not now!" said Vanessa.

"Sorry!" Jennifer whispered, stepping back.

Vanessa turned back to address Mr. Holman. "JP has been thoroughly reprimanded, and placed on a three-month suspension. But, with all fairness, he does suffer from bipolar disorder. He seemed to have been experiencing an allergic reaction to a new medication that day. He's apologized profusely, to both me, and Maya. Whom by the way, was a little tipsy that morning; those two, set a bad example. I mean, who has a glass of wine every morning!"

Mr. Holman pulled up another clip, from a surveillance camera inside The Grand. It showed Jason Garcia, stretching one of his clients, on the stretching table. All of the sudden, she begins massaging his penis. Jason pauses, looks around and continues stretching.

Mr. Holman fast-forwarded the clip, showing Jason getting a hand-job at a comical rate of speed. Vanessa began seething with anger, shaking her head. *I'm going to kill him.*

"Now, do you see what we're dealing with, Ms. Todd?" Asked Mr. Holman. "This isn't just one incident. There is a pattern of inappropriate and perverse behavior going on under your management."

"Why, I was unaware you received this tape?" Vanessa said, glaring at Mr. Richards, unsure how he got this tape without her knowing about it. "This is an interdepartmental incident that we have been investigating. The employee will be terminated shortly."

"But isn't he your top income earner?" Asked Jacob.

"Yes but—"

"Then wouldn't it be prudent for you to keep him in line instead of just firing him?" Jacob added. "After all, your numbers depend in part on his numbers."

"Yes I suppose," Vanessa attempted to explain, "but—"

"Then I advise you keep him on board until you can find a suitable replacement for the lost income." Said Jacob.

"I agree," said Mr. Holman. "We are in a precarious position, and as much as I hate to say it, disrupting cash flow is not tenable at this time. There is too much uncertainty. That kind of behavior is intolerable and would usually be a terminable offense, but under the circumstances—"

"This is the incompetence I'm talking about." Thomas interrupted. "What other company worth its salt, would put up with these shenanigans?"

Jacob raised his finger, while reading through Vanessa's projections. "These numbers, show a ten percent increase in membership sales, this past quarter alone."

Vanessa nodded her head, in agreement.

Jacob looked up, "And, projecting another four to five percent increase, going into the spring and summer. If these numbers pan out, that would be quite impressive."

"Impressive or not the Grand's image is at stake!" Barked Mr. Richards, "How come we never hear of Tiffany's, or The Ritz Carlton going through something like this?"

"Please Thomas, let's maintain our composure." Mr. Holman replied. He paused, for a moment to look through the numbers. "You're right Jacob, these projections are more than satisfactory. However, if this story comes out, I'm afraid these numbers won't mean anything. Any suggestions?"

"If I may…" Vanessa ventured.

"Are we seriously going to listen to this, right now?" Mr. Richards fumed.

Mr. Holman nodded his head at Vanessa.

"Unbelievable." Mr. Richards added, sorely.

Vanessa ignored him. "First, I would take any and all measures, to prevent that story from going out. We don't need this kind of attention right now, and besides there is no proof to these allegations. It's all hearsay. We should threaten to sue them for libel if they print such a specious, speculative story. Second, I would track down their source, make an example of them, and go after them with every legal resource at our disposal. We need to send the message that we are not to fair game, to be messed with, and more importantly that the Grand is not for sale. I suggest we start with Fit Corp. They're the ones who would benefit most from a scandal like this."

Mr. Richards clapped his hands, sarcastically. "*Bravo*! Looks like we got this all figured out."

Mr. Holman and Jacob both looked at him incredulously. "Unfortunately, nothing about what you just said is going to fix what is fundamentally wrong here. Look Stuart, the longer we keep going like this, the sooner we'll be acquired. We put in too much time, energy, and money trying to prevent the gym from going under; when we all know that it's almost inevitable at this point." He held up his folder. "Now with these numbers, we have an opportunity to come out on top. But, if we keep her on, we'll be shooting ourselves in the foot. And in six months, we'll be in the same situation, only we'll be in a weaker position financially. Come on Stuart, we discussed this, terminate her."

Jacob looked at Mr. Richards, and pointed at Vanessa. "As much as I hate to disagree, Thomas, she has a point." He shifted his glance to Mr. Holman. "She is also a big part of why the Grand has made such a strong comeback, these past four years. Whether, we end up selling or not, she's done an excellent job. With that said, I can have the legal department look into the story; To see if there's any way to delay The New York Post story, until we can figure out who's responsible for these accusations."

Mr. Holman leaned back in his chair, weighing what Jacob and Mr. Richards had each just said.

Mr. Richards looked, at the both of them, with contempt, "With all due respect, gentlemen, but have we gone stark fucking mad?"

Vanessa watched Thomas with a quiet smugness as he unraveled in front of everyone. His attempts to get her terminated had backfired, while calling his credibility to sit on the board of directors into question.

Mr. Holman leaned forward, and looked back at Mr. Richards, dismissively. "If you've quite finished Tom, I'd like to move forward now."

Stuart stood up, and began pacing around the table. "Taking in everything that's been said so far and giving it due consideration. I've come to the conclusion that we cannot disregard everything Vanessa has done for the Grand, because of some baseless rumor that she quite likely, had no way of preventing. I also can't be solely responsible for this decision, especially given the numerous oversights that *have* occurred, under her management. I propose that we bring this to a vote."

"Just minutes ago, we voted to fire the current management!" Said Mr. Richards, frustrated by the turn of events. "And now we're voting again, what's the point?"

Mr. Holman sat back down, calmly. "You're grievances are duly noted, Tom. We can continue this discussion in my office later if you feel dissatisfied with the methodology. For now, in lieu of this new information, we will hold another vote."

Mr. Richards rolled his eyes. Stuart looked him, square in the face. "I believe, I have made myself, perfectly clear, *Mr. Richards.* Is that the case?"

Mr. Richards nodded reluctantly.

"Very well." Mr. Holman continued. "Yea or Nay for keeping the current management. All those in favor."

Jacob and Mr. Holman both raised their hands "Yea."

Mr. Holman continued. "All those against."

"Nay" said Mr. Richards, feeling defeated.

"The Yeas have it." Mr. Holman stated, dutifully. "But under the condition, that this story goes away and the Grand's reputation remains mostly intact." He looked at Vanessa. "And Vanessa, you will make sure those projections are met. You have until the next quarterly meeting. If our conditions are not met, we will be forced to ask for your resignation. Is everything clear, Ms. Todd?"

"Yes. Thank you, Mr. Holman. We won't let you down." Vanessa said, relieved.

"I sincerely hope so. We're taking a big chance here." Mr. Holman replied.

"I will prepare a contingency plan in the likelihood that this blows up in our faces." Mr. Richards added, sneering at Vanessa.

Vanessa stood up. "Well then, gentlemen, always a pleasure." She shot a snarky glance at Mr. Richards. "If that is all, I really must be getting back to work."

"Good day, Ms. Todd, and good luck." Said Mr. Holman.

"Until next quarter." Said Jacob.

"Thank you both. Mr. Richards, I hope you have a lovely day as well."

Mr. Richards ignored Vanessa as she walked out of the boardroom. He stared out the window with his arms crossed, almost pouting. Jennifer walked over, gathered her things and followed Vanessa out, closing the door behind her.

"You own the board indeed, Mr. Richards," said Vanessa snidely, as she stepped onto the elevator.

13

Caught by the Short and Curlies

The next morning, Vanessa sat in her office scouring through the New York Post, looking for anything about the Grand. She went through the whole paper twice and couldn't find a single mention. *Well done Mr. Feinberg, well done.*

There was a soft knock on the door. "Come in!" Vanessa said, putting down the paper.

Jennifer popped her head in, "Did you see? There was nothing in the paper! Such good news!"

"Yes, I'm well aware Miss Diego." Vanessa replied, hiding her own elation. "How can I help you?"

"Oh, um... you asked me to find Jason."

"Yes, send him in, please."

Jennifer closed the door. A few seconds later, the door popped open again, and Jason strode in purposefully.

"Top o' the morning to ya! Lovely day we're having, not that you'd know, because there are no windows in here. You know, it's important to get some sunshine during the day, it helps with uh... Vitamin D —so look, are you gonna fire me?"

"Sit down Jason." Vanessa said.

"If it's all the same, I'd rather stand." Jason said. "I'd like to hold on to some of my dignity, instead of sitting down and being told I'm fired."

"Sit down!" Vanessa said, vexed.

"Woah-kay, no problem." Jason sat.

Vanessa stared at him without saying a word. He sat there for a moment, waiting to hear what she had to say. Squirming in his seat, getting increasingly uncomfortable with the awkward silence.

"How 'bout those Brooklyn Nets huh? It looks like they're putting together a good squad this year." He said, breaking the ice. "The

Knicks though, talk about a lousy—"

"Why can't you be quiet?" Vanessa interrupted, annoyed.

"What? I can be quiet! I'm the best quiet person I know. In fact, I'm so qui—"

"Shut up!" Vanessa said, pursing her lips. "I didn't call you in today to fire you."

Jason sighed in relief. "Whew! I thought this was it."

Vanessa shot him a mean glare.

"And I should shut up now," Jason said, gauging her reaction.

"I'm not sure if you were aware," Vanessa continued, "but Fit Corp is secretly trying to sabotage our efforts; To takeover our position in the fitness industry. I think they're attempting a takeover." She stood up from her desk and started pacing around the room.

"I had no idea!" Jason said, pretending. "Is that why you've been so bitchy—er, preoccupied lately?"

"My demeanor toward you has nothing to do with what's been going on. I do however, expect all my trainers to behave with the upmost professionalism, and to not undermine my authority."

"I'm not sure what you're getting at here." Jason said. "I'm an exemplary employee."

"Jason you were caught, on camera, receiving manual sex in the stretching area. What do you, have to say for yourself?"

Embarrassed, Jason shrank into his seat. "You saw that huh? I am, so sorry. It was all so unexpected. I didn't have time to process what was going on. It was a mistake. It'll never happen again, that I can promise."

"Really... that's your response?" Vanessa walked to the door. "I'm giving you a chance, to redeem yourself; And all you can say is you didn't have time to process a hand going down your pants; Pulling out your junk, and stroking it in public."

Jason stammered, "Uh... well... um."

Vanessa locked the door, "This is a terminable offense. You realize that?"

"But you're not, terminating me, so... " Jason said, unsure about what was happening.

Vanessa walked back around her desk, and sat down. "Hence, why we are here. You see, I thought long and hard about it. And I realized that firing you doesn't make the problem go away. If anything, it only makes my job, harder."

Vanessa looked Jason, straight in the face. "So I've decided to overlook this incident."

Jason sat up in his chair. "That is so cool of you. I really appreciate this second chance, and—"

"However, you do realize, there has to be consequences." Vanessa interrupted.

"So, I'm to be punished! *Ooh,* wait... where's your finger?" Jason said, looking around in his chair. He turned back, to see if he could possibly get Vanessa to smile.

Vanessa quietly seethed. "You're inability to act serious for just one minute, is not unlike a disability. I genuinely think you may have a personality disorder."

"Oh I'm definitely within the spectrum, somewhere between arrogant asshole and a Republican. I blame the patriarchy." Jason joked. "Oh... I see what I did there. I made an excuse for my behavior, that's another one of my character flaws."

"You need therapy."

Jason laughed. "You're probably right, but my awesomeness forbids anything that requires me to be vulnerable. Besides, therapists think they know everything but they're really the most fucked up people in the world; they're pompous, grandiose, degenerates with a hard on for people in dire circumstances.

Remember Dr. Ralph Finklestein? He was the sweetest guy, worked out hard, always on time. Turns out he was busted, for overcharging his corporate clients and possessing kitty-porn."

Vanessa gasped, "What? Child pornography!?"

"No that's kiddie porn, I'm talking about *kitty* porn! Meow, meow? Don't ask me what that is exactly, but it gives a new meaning, to the term pussy lover."

Vanessa winced, in disgust, "Must you be so *eloquent,* in your descriptions?"

"I'm sorry. I tend to blather, when I'm about to be strong armed into something I know I'm going to regret." Jason fired back. "But let's continue, I'm sure this will be great."

Vanessa sneered. "As I was saying, there needs to be retribution for your disregard of the rules. I had in mind, an indefinite probationary period."

"Probationary?"

"Under strict conditions, of course."

"How strict?"

"Look, Jason." Vanessa said, sitting back in her chair. "The Grand is in a delicate situation—"

"Delicate?"

"On one hand, we have the opportunity to expand globally. We would have gyms in every major city around the world. New York City would be our flagship. That means new facilities, new clients, and new opportunities. You could be a part of that."

Jason beamed, imagining the gym full of hot women from all over the world.

"On the other hand," Vanessa continued, "if another major scandal breaks or if we can't keep our revenue growth strong, our stock price will plummet, Fit Corp steps in, and buys up our outstanding shares in a hostile takeover. Best-case scenario, means most senior staff get replaced, salaried employees become part-time, and hourly wages get slashed."

"What kind of scandal are you talking about?" Jason asked, uneasy.

"Do you know anything about the steroid trafficking rumors going around?"

"Yeah, but they're just rumors, right?"

"Maybe so, but these *rumors* are trouble. If we don't come up with an explanation, it's going to be all over the tabloids. We can't have that sort of negative publicity."

"I don't know anything. Look, just because you see a few dudes, walking around, getting really jacked, doesn't mean they're on 'roids. It may just mean that your trainers are doing a hell of a job, ever consider that?"

"You trainers are so full of yourselves. Always taking credit for someone else's hard work. You watch people exercise and count reps while they endure your sadomasochistic tendencies. Only a sick mind would call that gratifying. Hell of a job my arse."

Jason raises an eyebrow, "Wow, part of me knows you just insulted me, but another part says 'shut up she's about to fuck you on this desk!' Does my intuition serve me well?"

Vanessa rolled her eyes. "I find you repulsive."

"That wasn't a clear, no."

"No! Absolutely not and never!"

"Okay, okay. Just have to be sure these days… I don't want to get our signals crossed. And if I recall correctly, you took advantage of my *sadomasochistic* services, from which you learned proper form, developed healthy habits, and got some pretty kick-ass results." Jason gestured at Vanessa body, indicating her fitness. "But you know what, I had nothing to do with that."

"You were just a means to an end," Vanessa quipped. "You were a tool—are a *tool*, and, if I recall correctly. I'm now the General Manager, and you're still an insubordinate employee. So let's continue, shall we? The New York Post has a credible source, saying that it has evidence of drug trafficking, here at the Grand."

Jason paused for a moment, trying hard to figure out what Vanessa was getting at. "So, I still don't get it, you think I'm selling drugs, or what?"

"Jason I know you better than to think there's any way you could pull that off. However, I'm positive that you can find out who is, if you don't already know. Besides, we both know I'm not the most popular person around the gym. If I start asking questions, nobody will talk."

"So, you think if I do it, people will talk?"

"You're much more of a people person than I am. You have a way about you that attracts others to you. People trust you, Jason." Vanessa said, trying to butter him up.

"Vanessa there is nothing special about me, although I can't argue with your logic. I come here everyday, do my job, and go home. Just because I'm a nice guy, doesn't mean anybody's going to open up to me about drug trafficking. I think you got the wrong person. I'm no, snitch."

"My goodness Jason, you don't how disappointed this makes me. I thought we were on the same team."

"You're asking me to betray people's trust."

"What's the bloody point of being trustworthy, if it puts you out of a job?"

"I don't know, maybe I'm finally standing up for something." He said.

"Right, right… well I'm sorry then, I must've given you the wrong impression; I'm really not offering you an option here." She said, ready to drop the hammer. "I'm going to put it to you another way, if you don't find out the sources of the rumors, concerning illegal drug trafficking in my gym. I'm going to assume it's you, who leaked the story. Then, I'm going to fire you, your buddies, and The Grand will pursue legal action against you, for slander."

Jason sat up. "Well shit just got real, didn't it?"

"Sure did! You can say, whatever you want, but this will be put on you. It doesn't matter, if you're not guilty. Corporate, will tie this up in court for so long. The legal fees, alone will ruin you financially. Not to mention, your reputation will be destroyed. Of course, you could counter sue but by the time you get your shite together, The Grand, will already be owned by Fit Corp. And, that's when the fun begins… so what do you say?"

Jason searched, for the words to fight back, but realized, that Vanessa had him right where she wanted him. He knew, she wasn't bluffing.

"Well, since you put it that way, how can I refuse?" Jason conceded. "It would appear that you've got me, by the short and curlies."

"Indeed." Vanessa said, smirking menacingly. "So you're on board then?"

Jason didn't reply. The look on his face, said it all. He was resigned to his charge.

"Wonderful! I'm so glad we can collaborate on this, feels like old times doesn't it?" Vanessa said, seductively walking over to him, putting her arm around him.

Jason began to feel sick, to his stomach. "Sure does feel like old times, everything except, for the blackmail part."

"Oh don't be such a wet blanket!" Vanessa whispered into his ear, rubbing his shoulders "I just need to be certain, that you're on my side, that you want the Grand to succeed. You do want the Grand to succeed, right?"

"The Grand is like a home to me." Jason gulped. "Nobody cares more about this place, than me."

"I know, Jason. That's why I'm promoting you to interim supervisor of personal trainers. How 'bout that for a plot twist?"

Surprised by Vanessa's announcement, "You can't be serious. I can't accept. I'll have to write boring budget reports, type emails, tell people what to do and stuff! That's too much responsibility. No, no, I can't. No way. Gives me angina, just thinking about it."

Vanessa stopped, massaging his shoulders. "It'll mean more hours, same pay. You will make sure, that trainers remain compliant, bring in money, render sessions, and you will report directly to me every day. Besides, you need more responsibilities. It'll keep you out of trouble."

"I can refuse." Jason said, defiantly.

"I suppose… but then you'll be letting everybody down. Do you want that on your conscience?"

Jason sighed.

"Everybody will know who is responsible, when they're out of a job—and so close to the holidays too." Vanessa shook her head. "I don't know about you, but I would not want to be in that position."

"But, you're the one in that position. You're the one who has to fire them."

"Technically yes, but you're the one who'll have to choose who goes and who stays. I on the other hand, only care about keeping this place open. I can replace you and the whole lot. It doesn't matter to me."

"It's not right, this is their livelihood we're talking about. These people have busted their asses here. They're not going to find another job in this economy, not making this kind of money. The trainers have put in so much into building their businesses—it's taken me years. Now, you're willing to take that away, for what? Just to get me to do what you want?" Jason said, trying to plead with her. "Get rid of me, I'm the one you want gone. I'm the one that rejected you remember? Leave them alone, where is your humanity?"

"Stop, being so bloody melodramatic, it's really unbecoming of you." Vanessa said. "Tugging on my heart strings will get you nowhere. Corporations lay people off everyday in this country. I'm trying to keep things from going south, but unfortunately I need help. I need access, access that you have. Do we have a deal?"

"Do I have a choice?" He said.

Vanessa stares at him smugly, without saying a word.

Jason sighed. "This is some straight, bullshit."

"I'm so glad we were able to come to an understanding!" Vanessa said, putting on her glasses and getting on her computer.

"So we're done here?" Jason asked.

"We are..."

Disheartened Jason got up, out of the chair and made his way to the door.

"Oh, and Jason one last thing before you go." Vanessa said, without looking up from her computer. "Congratulations, on your new promotion. I have a feeling that you won't disappoint."

Jason opened the door, pausing. "You know something, we may not have had hate sex on your desk today, but you still managed to fuck me real good." He walked out and closed the door.

14

It's all Coolio

Bex sat in The Grand's Café, with her headphones on, scarfing down her lunch; While listening to a new mix she'd been working on, before her next client. She'd been training people nonstop all morning, and was eager to sit in peace.

Tommy, however saw Bex and approached her table with his tray of food. He smiled wide, and waved hello. But, Bex barely acknowledged him, feigning a friendly smile before going back to devouring her second breakfast. She could see Tommy from the corner of her eye, hovering over her, trying to get her attention. Finally, she looked back up and saw him pointing to the empty seat in front of her.

She hesitantly took off her headphones.

"Is anybody sitting here?" Tommy asked.

"No, but..." she answered curtly, hoping he wouldn't sit down.

"Cool." He said, pulling out the chair. "What's up, what's good in the hood? I feel like we haven't spoken, in so long."

"Not long enough." She mumbled, under her breath.

"You know, we missed you the other night, you should've come out with us."

"I've been busy with work, and music. Although, I would've loved to have seen you get your ass kicked."

"Wow..." Tommy winced. "...That's not fucked up, at all."

Bex saw that she had hurt Tommy's feelings. "Oh come on, I'm kidding."

"I knew that." Tommy said, trying to let it roll off his shoulders. "Did Jay tell you?"

"Yeah, it's a good thing you got out when you did."

"Crazy Mike ain't shit. I could've taken him."

"Uh huh, okay Jackie Chan." She said, sarcastically. "This is why

I don't hang with you fuckers. You're always getting into some bull-shit that almost gets you killed."

"Not… always." Tommy said, thinking back.

"You guys need to grow up." Bex said, finishing up her meal.

"What do you mean? We're mature, well I'm mature." Tommy said, "Wow, this is so not how I thought this conversation would go."

"What are you talking about?" asked Bex.

"I thought I'd come over here, be all charming and stuff, ask you out on a date, you know. Some dinner maybe"

Bex sighed. "Look dude, I like you. You're a nice guy…" Tommy braced for the big *but*. "But… I don't date people from work, it's too complicated. Besides, I prefer to be alone. I'm better suited for it. Don't take it personal, okay. It's time for me to go, I have client in five minutes." She stood up and gathered her things. "See ya later, hey we still cool?"

"Yeah, we're cool, I'm cool, it's all coolio…" Tommy said, as Bex walked away. "Yep. See you on the frontlines. I'll just sit here." Tommy sat there, staring at his half eaten sandwich.

Martha Gladwell cackled from two tables away, having watched the whole scene. "Hee, hee… fucking loser."

15

I'm an Asshole.

Still reeling from his meeting with Vanessa, Jason grabbed his coat and stormed out of the gym, almost running over Mandy, who was also walking out.

"Oh, hi!" He said, holding the door after he realized who she was. "I almost ran you over."

"Not likely, I have a yogi body, but I carry the momentum of a train, so you better be careful." Mandy said, laughing.

"How ya doin', which way are you walking?" Jason asked.

"North, through Central Park." She answered.

"Perfect! I have a client around there, I'll walk with you."

"Alright…" She said.

It was a chilly November afternoon. Most of the leaves had fallen to the ground, dotting the great lawn with shades of red, yellow, and orange. A man with a saxophone, stood underneath the archway of a bridge. He played a classic love song that echoed, through the trees. The branches danced in the wind, as if they were in tune with the melody, just waving, back and forth, up and down.

Jason walked up and put a dollar in the musician's instrument case. The musician smiled and nodded in appreciation, without missing a note. Jason gave him a thumbs-up, as he and Mandy walked through the bridge's archway. Mandy had noticed that Jason wasn't being as chatty, as usual. She suspected something might be troubling him.

"You know, I never realized, you were such a great conversationalist." She joked.

"Huh?" Jason replied, preoccupied with Vanessa's ultimatum.

"Something's on your mind. I can tell, you've been kind of quiet?" He looked over at her. "… That obvious, huh?"

"Yeah, usually you're a lot more interesting to talk to." She said, poking fun at him.

Jason laughed, trying to play it off. "Oh really?"

"No really, is everything okay? You look like you lost your puppy."

Jason sighed, "I'm not sure… it's kind of complicated."

"What, are you having girl problems?"

Jason looked up at her, and smiled. *You have no idea.*

"No its not that. I just have a lot of shit going on right now, that's all. Stuff that I can't process at the moment. I hope I'm not coming off like a wet blanket."

"Oh no, it's fine, must be serious."

"You could say that." He said, realizing that he was squandering an opportunity to bond with Mandy. Who seemed, genuinely concerned about him.

"You'll figure things out." She said.

"Thanks… You know what though. I am acting a bit aloof, it'll be fine." Jason said, snapping out of his somber mood. "How about you, what's going on in Mandy world, these days? Did you notice that? How I subtly deflected, changing the subject? Good right? I'm like a ninja of subtle deflection. Segueing into different moods, I'm like a moody chameleon."

Jason pretended do some martial arts, trying to make Mandy smile, leading her away from his problem.

"Ha! More like a subtle ninja of B.S." Mandy joked.

Jason pretended to block a punch, "Ha ha, I deflected that too."

Mandy giggled. "Stop it."

She punched him in the shoulder. Jason rubbed it, pretending to be injured. "Ow! Should've seen that punch coming. I have dishonored my family, and shamed my ancestors. I must now fall on my ninja of subtleness sword." He said, patting his pockets, "Hmm, you wouldn't happen to have a ninja sword, on your person?"

"Um, I'm pretty sure, only Samurais fall on their swords." Mandy said.

Jason paused. "Huh… you sure about that?"

"Yeah."

"Well, in that case…" Jason snatched the hat off Mandy's head and took off running.

"Oh come on, it's cold!" She said, taking off after him.

He ran off the path onto a dirt trail, weaving in and out of some trees trying to lose her, but she quickly caught up.

Surprised by her speed, he turned around trying to out run her.

"Holy shit, you're fast!"

Jason, unable to see where he was going, tripped and fell over a tree root, tumbling into a pile of dried leaves and landing flat on his back. Mandy, unable to stop in time, tripped over Jason, falling on top of him. They both laughed uncontrollably, throwing piles of leaves at each other. Mandy lunged at him, pinning him to the ground, but he easily rolled her over, breaking free. He grabbed her by the arms, pulling her in close to make her stop. She struggled to free herself, but fatigue quickly set in, as she tried to catch her breath, from laughing so hard. Jason held her firmly, but gently in place, giggling at her futile attempts to break free. Exhausted, from trying to wiggle out, Mandy finally ran out of steam and succumbed to his pin. Jason held her, staring deep into her eyes, trying figure out if it was just a ruse, and she was about to counterattack. Slowly but cautiously, he began to release his grip. Mandy didn't move she just lay there, breathing heavily. She looked back into his dark eyes, wondering what all the fuss was about. He wasn't barbaric, or sleazy, the way JP said. She felt safe and warm in his arms, like nothing could harm her.

Jason could feel the warmth of her breath, on his face, and the rapid beat of her heart against his chest. For a split second, it felt as if time was standing still. They drifted closer and closer, being pulled together, by some irresistible force. Until their lips, were just millimeters away. The steam of their breath combined, condensing, into a light haze. Humidifying the dry air around them. *This must be what magic feels like.*

Suddenly, Mandy snapped out of the hypnotic trance, and backed away. "Can I get my hat back?" She asked.

Jason smiled, "Whatever you say, just don't hurt me."

Mandy grabbed a handful of leaves, and shoved them into his face. She snatched her hat back, and got up. Jason slowly got up, and started dusting himself off, spitting out pieces of twigs and leaves.

"Ugh, was that organic? Because, it tasted organic!"

"Come on!" She said, taking him by the arm. "You're gonna be late, for your next client."

"It really wasn't bad, I especially liked the earthy flavor. Crunchy, not too woody with just a hint of rat excrement." Jason laughed.

Jason and Mandy, walked back up to the road that led up to Cat Hill. A part of the park, where people, went to run and bike. The hill itself was named after the large sculpture of a cat, perched atop a boulder on the side of the road. Looking down over the ledge, as if it were getting ready to pounce on an unsuspecting victim.

"Ugh… I'm starting to get flashbacks." Jason said, as they ascend up the winding road.

"Why do you say that?" Mandy asked.

"This is the spot where I always run out gas, when I jog." He said. "It's terrible, you should see me. I start out strong at the beginning, but then, by the time I reach the top. I'm a hot mess. I'm out of breath, clutching my chest. I look like I'm going into cardiac arrest. It's bad."

Mandy looked back at the road, it wasn't a very long distance. "Really… it's not that bad. You just need to run more, that's all."

"Ugh…" Jason replied. "Did I mention, that I hate running. It's like bad medicine. I take the minimal dose, only because I have to."

Mandy laughs. "Well if I weren't so booked, I'd run with you."

"So I take it, things are going well for you, at the gym then?"

"Yeah I guess. All my classes are super full—which is great, don't get me wrong. I'm happy about it, but now I'll be teaching all of JP's classes while he's away." She said. "I'm not going to have time for anything else."

"That is a good problem to have, there are a lot of good people out there, with no jobs at all. Struggling to get by everyday, just to put food on the table. Waiting for things to get better. These huge banks and finance guys really fucked us, and now we have to pay for their mistakes. I count my blessings everyday, I have a job." He lamented.

"Careful what you say, my fiancé is one of those *finance guys*." Mandy quipped.

"He would work for them… But you know what I mean, it's just not fair, that's all."

"No, you're absolutely right, things are fucked up. I should stop complaining."

"It's okay, say what you want. This is America. The subject though, gets me heated." Jason said, trying to move away from the subject. "So how is my old friend JP?"

"He's fine…" Mandy said unconvincingly. "Is it me, or is there something off, about him?"

"J.P.! No, no he's fine!" Jason said sarcastically. "You know, in a psychotic, narcissist, who may snap one day, and go on a rampage, kind of way."

Mandy laughed. "He is psychotic, isn't he?"

"Let's just say J.P. will only be happy in J.P.'s world. He makes Kanye, look humble; know what I mean?"

Mandy laughed so hard, she snorted.

Jason stopped, "What the fuck, was that?"

"Excuse me, I snort sometimes, when I laugh too hard."

"That was a snort? My god, I thought you were having a stroke." He said, laughing even harder. "I though I was going to have to call a paramedic, jeez!"

Mandy grabbed Jason's arm, she laughed again. "Stop! You're going to make me snort again."

Jason found her snort endearing, "I'm getting the impression that's it's gonna be hard, being friends with you. You realize that, right? Does Spencer like the strange sounds that come out of you, because if he doesn't, I'll take you off his hands. Poor guy probably hates taking you to see Romantic comedies."

"He dreads it, by the way his name is Steven." Mandy said, catching her breath.

"Right, Steve the trader."

"Steven Ashworth III, Junior VP at Harlow Squire." Mandy said in a sarcastic snooty tone. "At least that's what it says on his business card."

"Oh, Harlow Squire makes me like him even more!" Jason said.

"You know he's out to get you."

"Who Spenc…err I mean, Steven?"

"No, J.P. He said it doesn't matter what you do, Vanessa is going to fire all the trainers. He'll see to it."

Jason feigned concern. "They won't do that. They can't do that. We make them too much money. They'd be shooting themselves in the foot."

"I know, but J.P. thinks Fit Corp should take over, and everyone should be replaced, especially you."

"Oh J.P., that ol' rascal," Jason said dismissively. "He's just expressing, his concern, for the gym."

Jason noticed the look of concern, on Mandy's face, and got serious for a moment. "Look, I know what they're trying to do, it does have me a little preoccupied."

"That's so unfair…"

"Unfair, maybe… but I'm definitely not without fault, in all of this."

"How?"

"Well I don't know how to tell you this, but I'm kind of an asshole."

Mandy looked at Jason confused, by what he was saying. "So you deserve to be fired?"

"Depends on your perspective, I guess." He said, "It's complicated, there's a lot of ins and outs, lot of layers."

"Well I've seen how you train, your clients. You're nothing but professional, attentive, extremely knowledgeable, and they all freakin' love you."

"Yes, yes that's all true, please continue. I crave the adulation." He said, laughing. "That's the asshole part, I'm talking about. Although, Vanessa and JP consider me narcissistic, mercurial, and immature."

"Don't forget brutish, barbaric, and fat." Mandy added.

"Ouch!" Jason said, loudly. "That doesn't sting at all, who said that?"

"JP." Mandy replied.

"I may be roguish, devilish even, but brutish… and fat?" Jason sucked in his stomach.

Mandy laughed. "So you're just cocky then?"

Jason shrugs his shoulders, with a smug grin on his face, walking with a little more swagger in his step.

"There's nothing wrong with being a little cocky, it exudes confidence." Mandy said.

"My sentiments, exactly." Jason replied. He stopped and looked into Mandy's eyes again, trying to see if his attitude had put her off.

Mandy smiled, for a moment. Then quickly looked down, at her watch. "Thanks, for walking me, all this way. Are you going to be late, for your client?"

"Nah, she can wait. So getting back to Steven—"

"Jason you're going to be late, for your client," Mandy interrupted. "I'll see you at the gym."

Mandy turned around and began to walk away, leaving Jason standing there. "Mandy wait…"

She turned around.

"It's true, I'm an asshole. I'm vain, I don't think of anybody but myself. I'm immature, probably out of shape. I purposely don't bother to re-rack the weights at the gym, because I know it pisses off Facundo. But, there's one more thing…" Jason walked toward Mandy.

"What's that?" Mandy asked, looking deeply into Jason's eyes as he approached her.

"I care." he said, softly.

"I know." Mandy replied. She kissed Jason on the cheek and began to walk away again. "Will I see you, at the gym tomorrow?"

"Everyday!" He said. *Slow your roll, Jay, she's engaged.*

16

Pet The Baby

It was 3:15, when Jason arrived to his 3pm appointment. He rang the doorbell. Dusted off the remaining twigs, and plucked the last bits of leaves, onto the plush carpet of The Beaumont East; A pre-war, luxury building, renowned, for its incredible views of Central Park. A four-bedroom apartment, at the Beaumont, is said to cost, at least five million dollars. Jason's, client owns the penthouse.

The sounds, of locks unlatching, could be heard, through the door.

A middle-aged, Jamaican woman, opened the door. Ms. Venetta had been, with the Pierce family, for a few weeks now, first as a mid wife, and now as a Baby Nurse. She stood in the doorway, staring at Jason, suspiciously, as to why he was there. Jason noticed she was holding a newborn baby; Face down, over her forearm, petting it. Like one would pet a cat, or small dog.

"What you want…?" Ask the woman.

Jason stood there for a moment, watching her pet this baby, "Um, is Mrs. Pierce here?"

"Who are you?"

"I'm her trainer. We have an appointment today." Jason replied, "Is that Teresa's baby? He's so new and wrinkly. What's his name?

"Franklin Titan Pierce."

"Titan huh, what's up little bud…"

"Shh, you'll wake the baby." Venetta interrupted, turning around, leaving the door open for him to enter.

"Mrs. Pierce! Ya traina's 'ere." She yelled, startling Jason.

"Thank you Venetta, send him in." Said a voice, coming from one of the bedrooms.

Venetta turned to Jason, looking him, up and down. "Ya 'eard da lady."

Jason cleared his throat, "Thank you."

He walked, through the long hallway of the foyer, across the massive living room, toward the doorway, leading to the bedrooms. "Uh Teresa, I'm kind of lost here." He said, trying to find his way.

"Hey!" Said Teresa, from behind, startling him.

She grabbed Jason, kissing him deeply, catching him off guard.

Teresa Stewart-Pierce was a tall, extremely beautiful, woman. In her youth, Teresa rode horses, in Equestrian competitions, at her family's country club in Connecticut. Later in college, she played competitive volleyball. Winning a national championship, with her team in the senior year. Then, for a few years after college, she began modeling for high-end lingerie companies. She became, pretty well known, in the modeling industry. But sadly, the shelf life, of a female model is a short-lived career. After deciding to retire from modeling at age twenty-seven, and much to the dismay of her parents, Teresa got married to Jonathan Wellington Pierce, her parent's former financial advisor; who was twenty-five years, her senior. Her parents embarrassed, by what they called a scandalous affair had to leave the country club, over the controversy. But Teresa, could care less, in fact she liked that her parents were uncomfortable. That was her way, of getting back at them, for not being there for her, when she was a kid.

"Hey… Teresa, it's great to see you." He said, trying to be subtle, and pull away.

"So what do you think?" She said, doing a turn, "Not bad for five weeks post partum."

"You're not kidding. It's like, you never had a baby, considering he looked like, he could've done some real damage, down there" He said, impressed with her figure.

"Oh please… My hips are huge."

"Yeah, it's called giving birth. Go easy on yourself, I know women who'd kill their third husband, to have your figure… literally."

"Well if that were true, why would I need you?" She said, jokingly.

"You kidding me, those hips are massive." He quipped.

Teresa playfully, punches him in the arm, turns around, and leads him to the workout area.

Jason got the resistance bands, and suspension trainer, out of his bag. He then, had Teresa do some dynamic stretches, while he set up the equipment. He watched her, carefully assessing her movements. Making sure she was able, to work out; Keeping in mind that, Doctors usually don't want women to exercise, for at least six weeks, after giving birth. But, Jason figured five weeks, is close enough. He then, instructed Teresa, to do some simple core exercises. In order to, re-acclimate her body to exercise.

"God! I feel so weak." She said, flustered at how awkward, her body feels.

"It's totally natural, you can't expect to do burpees, right after child birth." Jason said.

"I know. It's just that, I've always been an athlete. I've never, not been able to do something. And now…"

Teresa's eyes began to well up, with tears.

"Whoa, hey, let me stop you, right there. Becoming, a mother is a great accomplishment. Your body goes through nine months of hell, in order for you to have that, little bundle of joy. Which, by the way is super adorable. I saw him on the way in."

"I thought he, was still napping." Said Teresa.

"No he's definitely napping, I didn't want to get too close. I don't think your nanny, likes me much."

"Don't mind Venetta, she's a sweetheart."

"Anyway, you have to recover." He said, trying to cheer her up. "It's like running a marathon… for nine months. You would never get back out and sprint the day after, right?"

"You're right." She said, "I also just think, I'm depressed. With Jonathan in prison, I'm just so overwhelmed."

"Yeah well, that'll do that to ya." Jason said, awkwardly. "When, does good ol' Johnny, get out of the slammer, anyway?"

"Well, if the Attorney General has his way. He'll be looking at, fifteen to twenty…" She replied.

Jason's jaw dropped. "Damn! Fifteen, to twenty years, holy shit, that's a rough stretch!"

"… Months." She said, correcting him.

"Wait… that's it? How did he, manage that?" he asked. "Because, I know if I were to scam people, out of millions dollars. I'd be doing a hard twenty, in a cell, with a guy named Booty Harrelson."

"Jonathan has the best lawyers in the country. He struck a plea deal, with the government."

"Well good for him, I guess." Said Jason, unsure about how he felt, about that.

"Do you think Jonathan's getting off easy?" Teresa asked, sitting next to Jason.

"What do I know, about the law, I'm no judge." He answered.

"Yeah, but you think it's not fair." She said, putting her hand on his thigh.

Jason took a deep breath, "It doesn't matter, what I think. I'm a nobody."

"Aw… you're not a nobody." She said, whispering in his ear.

"I'm not?"

Teresa nibbled on Jason's earlobe. "Of course, you're not."

Jason's jaw tensed, as he gulped nervously. He turned, to look at her. "Um, you have another set of push-ups."

Her hand moved up his thigh, between his legs. Jason cleared his throat, looking around. *Ahem,* "We're just gonna do this right here, with doors open and everything huh?" *Holy shit! I can't do this. Wait, what is wrong with me?*

Jason looked over at the entrance. He envisioned Venetta, standing by the doorway. Shaking her head in disapproval, as she pets the baby.

Jason jumped up, "Uh, hey! We still have more to do!"

"I know… lots more." Teresa said, sticking her hands down his sweats. She noticed the mortified look on his face. "Are you okay?"

"Yeah, I'm fine it's just that, you have a lot going on right now, and I don't want to take advantage…"

Teresa snapped out of her seductive tone, and pulled her hands out of his pants. "You're rejecting me? God, I'm such an idiot!"

"It's not a rejection. I just want to make sure you're really okay. There's no need to get upset."

"You don't want me anymore." She said, tearing up. "You think I'm disgusting!"

"No, no, no… You're not disgusting at all."

Jason stared at the entrance, hoping Venetta wouldn't come. "You're fucking hot, extremely attractive! I'd love nothing more than to pin you up against the wall, and play baby roulette. But what you really need right now, is a friend. This thing, you and me have is special, for me it's more than just about sex. You know what I mean?"

Teresa began to calm down, as she breathed deeply, "You're right, I am a little crazy right now."

"That's good, see… shit is too nuts. Are we good? Can I finish kicking your ass, into shape now?"

Teresa wiped her nose, with her towel, and laughed. Jason gave her a long and loving hug. Reassuring, her that everything's going to be okay. He then motioned toward the ground. An indication that, Teresa should prepare for the next, round of exercises.

"Get your fine ass, on the floor. I want twenty, hip extensions."

Teresa got down on her back, bent her knees, and lifted her hips off the ground.

"I have an appointment, with my Doctor tomorrow. I think I'm going to ask her, about what medications; I should take, to threat this Post Partum depression.

"You should see your Doctor. Although, I'm of the mind, that some *D*, will do you ya a lot of good." He said.

"*D*! What are you talking about?" Teresa asked, wondering what he was implying.

"You know, vitamin D. It's good for your mood, calcium absorption, and bunch of other shit."

"Oh, Okay."

"Anyway, I'm glad you're seeing your Doctor." Said Jason.

17

Highly Inappropriate Harvey

Matt kneeled beside his client, who had just finished a round of planks. "Okay Harvey, you're all set. Good workout today. You keep getting stronger, pretty soon you're not going to need me anymore." Matt said, handing him a towel.

Harvey took the towel and wiped himself off. "I was running around in the jungles of Vietnam, before you were a tickle in your daddy's ball sack. I don't need any of this shit!" He snapped.

"Glad to see, the endorphins kicking in." Matt quipped.

"Did I ever tell you the story, about how I singled-handedly saved an orphanage, from being overrun by the Viet Cong?" Harvey asked.

"No you haven't… oh wait, only about twelve times, but who's counting?" Matt said, busting Harvey's chops.

"You see, that's the problem with you Millennials. Always thinking, you know everything!"

Matt got up and walked toward the Men's locker room, Harvey followed closely behind.

"I don't think, I'm all that. Well, maybe just a little." Matt thought, "So, what do you got going on, for the rest of the weekend, Harv?"

Harvey grunted. "Eh, I'm going out to dinner with the Mrs. tonight, I'm really not looking forward to it."

Matt headed over to his locker. "Really, why is that?"

"Because, all of her friends from her Alma Mater are going to be there. Crowing to each other about their precocious grandchildren." He said.

Matt sat on a bench, opened his locker, and began going through his gym bag. "So, what's the problem? Don't feel like, bragging about the grandkids?"

"I don't have any... " Said Harvey.

"Oh, well I guess you'll have to wait until your son settles down." Said Matt.

"Yeah, that'll happen." He said, sarcastically.

"Why do you say it, like that?" Matt asked.

"Because my son's a fudge-packing, pillow biter." Harvey replied.

"Whoa, whoa… Harvey, people can hear you." He said, looking around to see if anyone was listening. "Harv, you can't talk like that."

"Who cares, I'm old. I didn't spend two years, stalking Charlie, through the muck. To come home, so I could pretend to care about everybody's feelings. What a bunch of Nancy crap."

"Still Harv, this isn't the military of 1969. People are more tolerant, these days." Matt said, pulling two pill bottles, out of his bag, and rolling them into the towel. "Besides, this stuff, will keep you young."

Matt handed the rolled up towel to Harvey. "Yeah, yeah… Too bad, it doesn't make my dick hard." said Harvey. He took the towel, extended his other hand, filled with cash, and shook Matt's hand. Exchanging the money discreetly.

"Thank you, very much sir, I appreciate the business. Don't forget, to take those, with a meal." Said Matt. "We on, for next week, right?"

"Yeah, yeah… By the way, that stuff I said about my son, doesn't mean I don't love him. He's always been a good kid, that's what matters right? Even if he does takes it in the ass." Harvey said, shuddering at the thought.

"Again Harvey, highly inappropriate." Matt said, unfolding the cash and counted it, as he walked out of the men's locker room. His phone buzzed, Matt folded the bills, put them in his pocket and pulled out his cell phone. The text was from Claire.

"Hey, I'm taking off, for a few days. Going to the Berkshires, for a yoga retreat.

A big, smile came over Matt's face. *This day just keeps getting better and better.*

18

How About Some Head Instead?

Jason sat, in the stairwell of the Grand, typing a text to Mandy.

Hey Mandy, thanks for walking with me yesterday. It was so nice, to talk to you. – J

He had just hit send, when the door to the stairwell, suddenly opened. Vanessa cautiously, walked into the stairwell. Scanning the area, warily making sure, no one else was around.

"There's no one here, I checked." said Jason, "Why can't we meet, in your office again?"

"No one knows that you're spying for me, not even Jennifer. She'll know something's up, if you keep coming, to my office everyday." Said Vanessa.

"You're right, sneaking into the stairwell everyday, isn't suspicious at all. If only, there was a device that could be used to send information…" Jason held up, his phone. Vanessa glared, at him.

"But, whatever… this is cool too." He quipped.

"Can you not be such a bloody asshole, all the time? It's exhausting." Vanessa said.

"A *bloody*, asshole that's a first… wait no it isn't. "

Jason's phone buzzed, it was Mandy.

No problem, it was nice.

Jason quickly texted back, while Vanessa kept talking.

I'm going that way again, today. Care to join?

He looked back up at a Vanessa, who was seething.

"I'm sorry, you were saying?" He asked.

"I understand, you have some information, for me?"

"Right, um… I have some information." Jason said, uneager to share. "I found this pill, in the locker room."

He pulled out, a small blue pill, from his hoodie pocket. Holding it out in the palm of his hand.

Vanessa put on her glasses, for a closer look, "What is it? Wait… that's an E.D. pill! I said steroids, Jay, steroids!"

"Yeah but, where there's limp dick pills, there has to be steroids."

"What are you talking about? One thing has nothing to do, with the other. Oh my fucking God! You're wasting, so much time, you moron!"

"I just figured, whoever is dealing dick pills. Also, has to be dealing, dope pills."

Jason could see, Vanessa's blood pressure rising, from the little vein, beginning to protrude, on her right temple. "I also heard, there was a transaction, of the monetary kind in the locker room, earlier today between two guys." He said.

Vanessa crossed her arms. "Go on."

"That's all I know." Jason replied.

"That's all—who told you this?" Vanessa demanded.

"Look divulging my sources, was not part of the deal. People won't trust me if I snitch them out. So, you're going to have to let me do this my way. Besides, my source won't tell me, either."

"Not even if I terminate you, for withholding information?" Vanessa said, threateningly.

"Sure, you could do that. Have fun, finding everything out yourself though. Especially, in such a crucial time." Jason smirked, roguishly. "Can we just be nice, to each other now?"

Vanessa rolled her eyes. "It's a good thing, for you, that I still need more proof. Same time, tomorrow then?" Vanessa turned, to leave.

Jason scoffs, "You know, with all this talk of firing people, making them pay and stuff, you sound like a stereotypical TV villain. So much, drama, mean-ness, and contemptuous disregard for your subordinates. For what, so you can look good, in front of the board. What do they have on you? Is *your* job on the line, do you get a bonus, for cutting cost, what's made you like this?"

Vanessa turned around, glaring at Jason.

"So, I'm just some evil bitch, bent on destruction is it? Some crazy woman, that doesn't make any sense, when she expresses any sort of anxiety. Incapable, of making a sound decision, despite the fact, that there are serious problems around here, regarding money and drugs. This place is being systematically sabotaged, so it can be taken over, by a company that will get rid of everyone who doesn't fit into their exploitative pay system. But, I'm the bad and hateful one? Your problem, is that you can't handle a strong, assertive, woman, in charge. Doing what is necessary, to keep this place a float. Your patriarchal perspective of women is archaic, sexist, and immature. Grow up Jason, this isn't TV land."

Vanessa stormed out of the stairwell, slamming the door behind her. Jason sat there for a moment, shaking his head. *Wow, drama much?*

Two quick pulses, from his phone notified him, of an incoming text.

"It was nice walking with you yesterday, but I don't think we should make it a thing. Don't think my fiancé, would appreciate it much."

Jason sighed. *Ugh… fucking fiancé!*

"Hey no worries, I figured, since you go up that way anyway. That we could…" he replied.

Jason stood up, putting his phone, in his pocket. He walked out of the stairwell, onto the gym floor, taking a deep breath; mentally preparing himself, for his next client. Who, just happened to be Vanessa's assistant Jennifer.

Jennifer was stretching, on the gym floor, wearing baggy plaid pajama-like pants. The kind people wear, when they're walking their dog, at 8 am on a Sunday morning. She also wore, a simple gray t-shirt, with The Grand's logo on it.

Jason walked, over to her. "Yes! She's here… are you ready to get serious, my lady?" He said, over dramatically.

Jennifer shyly, raised her hand, "… ready."

"Are you ready to sweat, burn, and work until your body gives out?" he said.

"Uh…" she uttered.

"Are you ready, to hand your body over to me, so that I can methodically, beat you up, break you down, and rebuild you; into a well-calibrated machine, that will lift, pull, and press anything, I throw at it?"

"Okay…"

Jason hugged her tightly "Shh… my child, rest your head on my bosom. For you have taken the first step, toward reclaiming your body."

He gently tried to place her head, on his chest. She resisted at first, but reluctantly gave in.

"Swear your fealty to me, and you shall rise, from the ashes of sweat. Into a bright, svelte phoenix, with ripped abs, and toned arm wings. You will conquer the reaches of the Earth, and beyond to— oh wait I got a text."

Jason abruptly released her, and pulled out his phone. It was a text, from Mandy

"How about some head instead?"

"Wha!" Jason said, shocked.

"What is it?" Jennifer asked.

"Uh… nothing, go warm up, on the bike. I'll be right with you." Jason insisted, as he texted, feverishly.

"But, I don't know how to—"

"Can't talk. Just pedal, I'll be right there. Shortly. Go!"

"I'll check the yes please box, where do you want to meet?

Jason hit send, as he walked, over to where Jennifer was warming up. He put his phone, back in his pocket.

First, Jason had Jennifer do some basic dynamic stretches; that prepared her musculoskeletal system for the day's work out. Then, he had her do some bodyweight squats, modified push-ups, and a set of standing rows.

"How do you feel?" Jason asked.

"Good." Jennifer said, catching her breath.

"Awesome, go grab a drink of water. Then come back, for round two."

Jennifer nodded, and walked over to the water fountain. Jason quickly, pulled out his phone. There was another text from Mandy:

"You tell me."

Giddy, Jason thought, for a moment. *Where can we fuck?*

He wrote back:

"There's an electrical room, on the 3rd floor, it's perfect. Meet you there, in fifteen minutes?

Jennifer walked backed over, "Okay, ready for round two."

"Alright, begin with a set of twenty, bodyweight squats." Jason said, preoccupied with his phone. It dinged, as he got a reply.

"Okay, but we would have to hurry. I have a lot of classes, to teach."

Jennifer finished the squats. "Alright, back to push-ups." Jason said.

Jennifer dropped down, and got into position. Her arms pressed into the floor, lifting her body up.

"Keep your head neutral, it's dropping too low, and keep your chin up." Jason said, not even looking at her. His eyes were fixed on his phone, as he texted Mandy.

"I got it covered, its quiet, out of the way, and no one goes back there. I'll have it all ready, cool?"

"Okay, I'll have ten minutes so..." Read, Mandy's reply.

"Gotcha." Grinned Jason.

Jason put his phone away, turned to Jennifer, who was still doing push ups. "Awesome set of push ups, Jen. Now let's do a quick set of burpees, then we'll wrap this up, okay?"

"Burpees? But what about the standing rows?" She asked.

"Burpees, will make you forget about standing rows, real quick. Besides, something's coming up, that'll require my undivided attention." Jason said, trying not sound, too devilish.

"Oh, okay... I can do these on my own, if you need to go." She said.

"No, I couldn't do that to you, abandoning you like this, that's wrong. Really though, you wouldn't mind?"

"Sure... go, I got this." Jennifer insisted.

"You're my hero Jen, I'll never forget you." Jason said, shaking Jennifer's hand. Grateful that she didn't seem, too bothered.

Jason left in a rush, looking at his phone, completely forgetting about Jennifer. She stood there for a moment, contemplating whether she should finish up with the burpees. As soon, as he was out of view, she decided it was too much work and headed for the locker room. She then paused, changed her mind, and went back to complete the workout.

Meanwhile, Jason skipped up the stairs, two, or three steps at a time. Racing to the 3rd floor, as fast as he could. He grabbed a yoga mat, a few towels, and some lotion from the massage rooms, along the way. *I'm the motherfuckin' man!*

Jason stormed into the electrical room, threw everything down, and began to clear the area of debris. He had ten minutes, to clean the room up, and have it ready for Mandy.

He pulled a tarp off some beams, and placed them out of the way. He piled some crates into a corner, placing the tarp over them, rolling the yoga mat out. Placing it on top of the crates, making it look like a makeshift bed. Hurriedly, Jason grabbed a broom and started sweeping, accidentally, disturbing a mouse nest.

"Mouse!" He shrieked, trying to clobber the rodents, with the broom. They scattered throughout the area, scurrying, under cabinet doors, cracks in the walls, and up pipes in the ceiling.

"They're gone." He said, relieved.

Finally, after all that, the secret rendezvous was ready.

Jason hurriedly, pulled off his clothes, throwing them into a corner. He then cupped his hand, placed it over his mouth, huffing and sniffing. To check, the quality of his, breathe. *Breathe, status good.*

He then, took the same hand, placed it his underwear, rubbed his groin, and sniffed. *Dick musk status… satisfactory.*

Jason grabbed the massage lotion, lathered himself thoroughly, preparing for Mandy's arrival.

The phone buzzed, *"Not sure, if I'll have time now."* Read Mandy's text.

Jason desperately texted, back, *"Don't worry, I won't make you late, everything is ready.*

He waited nervously, for her reply, wondering if she'd still come. The thought of Mandy, and him having sex, began to give him, an erection. His phone buzzed again.

"Okay on my way, but keep in mind, I'll be in a rush."

"Yes!" Jason shouted.

"It's all good here, the room is ready." Read his reply.

He put on the romantic music station app, on his phone, attempting to create a romantic ambience. Jason then swallowed, the erection pill he found. Lay back, on the bed of crates, and began masturbating. Imagining, what he and Mandy will do to each other. He could feel his penis getting hard, as he stroked it. Images of kissing Mandy, on the lips filled his head. She kissed on the lips, then on then neck, then down to the chest and stomach, then…

All of the sudden, the door to the electrical room swung open. And three firemen, with pick axes, burst in.

Jason jumped up, from the crates, trying to cover his erection. "What the fuck! What's… going on?"

The firemen stared at him, standing there almost naked. One of them stepped forward. "We received a call, about a fire in the electrical room, in this building."

Facundo enters behind the firemen, curious about what was going on.

"No fire here." said Jason, totally flushed with embarrassment.

The firemen looked around the room. Then back at Jason, who was scampering about, picking up his clothes. Suddenly, a mouse fell from the sprinkler pipe, landing on Jason's shoulder.

He shrieked, "Mouse!" He dropped everything and ran out of the room. The three firemen and Facundo just stood there perplexed, by what was going on.

19

I Was Hoping We Could Hang out Tonight.

Tommy, Jason, and Facundo sat on a futon in Matt's cramped studio apartment. Matt sat on a stool, next to the kitchenette, eating chicken wings and pizza. Bex sat on the floor, with her headphones on, tuned out. She was DJing some chillwave house music, bobbing her head to the beat. Tommy glanced at her occasionally, hoping to make eye contact between bong rips.

Facundo played videogames on Matt's gaming console, continually getting himself killed, muttering obscenities under his breath. Jason was on his third beer, as he watched Facundo play, trying not to think about what happened earlier in the electrical room.

Tommy ripped the bong, held his breath for a few seconds then coughed out a thick plume of white smoke. He offered the bong to Jason, but Jason declined. He then, offered it to Facundo, who reached for it while still playing with one hand.

"You can't play with one hand. Give me that." Jason said, snatching the bong from Tommy.

"He can't play period." Tommy laughed.

"I still can't believe she did you like that man!" Matt said, from the kitchenette.

"Me neither man!" Said Tommy. "It's awful. How do you feel? Angry, embarrassed, betrayed?"

"… Like shit." Said Jason as he exhaled smoke.

"Yeah man." Tommy agreed. He looked over at Bex, who was scrolling through music, on her computer.

Facundo mumbled incoherently, in Spanish.

Jason sat up. "I can't help it Facundo! It's a design flaw of mine. I'm just a hopeless romantic, I guess."

Tommy patted Jason on the back, and then reached for the bong.

Matt wiped his mouth, tossed his napkin, into an overflowing trash bin. The napkin, bounced off, hitting the floor, "Gotta admit though, that was a good prank."

"Good is an understatement," said Jason. "That was on some next level, diabolical shit."

Jason snatched the bong back from Tommy, and ripped it. "I mean look, I can appreciate a quality burn, but what the fuck was that about?"

Facundo mumbled.

Jason glanced back, at him. "I was a complete and utter gentleman, Facundo; Un caballero." Facundo rolled his eyes.

"There needs to be retribution. You have to retaliate, an eye for an eye!" Said Tommy, reaching for the bong.

"Wow, really children?" Bex interrupted. "What if Jay was just being his usually charming self and Mandy saw right through it?"

Tommy put down the bong, and made a face, as if he had been planning not to hit it.

Matt coughed. "Damn dawg, she said, you deserved it."

"Can't argue with her logic." Jason replied. "But Mandy, doesn't know me like that. And besides, she's different."

A collective jeer came from everyone, in the room.

Aw! Whatever, Jay!

Facundo shook his head, dismissively.

Matt threw another crumpled napkin at Jason. "Look Jay, every girl is different, like a snowflake. And then, you bag 'em and tag 'em. That's how you do."

"That's not crude, at all Matt." Bex said, snappily.

"No disrespect B." Matt replied. "I'm just saying. Jay is acting, like he's on some fairytale, shit again. We all know where it leads."

Jason looked over at Tommy, "Am I not sitting, right here? Why are they talkin' about me, like I'm not here?"

Tommy ignored him, while perusing Matt's video game collection.

"Look who's talking, Mr. Casanova, para ninguna parte." Jason, pointed to Matt. "You and Claire barely acknowledge each other."

Matt picked up his third slice of pizza and shoved it in his mouth, "Yeah, but I did four years, of hard time with her, it's different."

Bex put the music on auto, took off her headphones, picked up her beer, and sat next to Jason. "Jay you need to admit it, you haven't always been a gentleman."

Jason looked at Bex. "Okay, okay, I admit it. I fall in love too easily, but I'm always respectful."

"It's hard to mess things up, when your longest relationship has only been a few days." Tommy chimed in.

"Et tu, Tommy, really." Jason said, "I feel like I'm being date shamed, by everybody. Help me Facundo."

Facundo mumbled a few words in Spanish.

"Exactly! Thank you, Facundo. The search for true love is *not* easy, but the journey *is* worth it. " Jason repeated, standing up from the couch. "You all need to listen to this man. He is a sage, wise, and spicy."

Tommy pointed to a game, on the shelf. "Oh shit you got Football Nation '15!" He said, excitedly.

Matt nodded, in agreement, "Yes…"

Tommy continued. "This is the one with your—"

"Yeah." Matt nodded again.

"Well shit, let's put it on!"

"Let's not." Matt said.

"What, why?" Tommy asked.

"Yeah Matt, why not? Still hating on your brother?" Said Jason.

"No. The game just sucks, that's all." Matt said sheepishly.

"Put this on Facundo!" Tommy insisted.

Facundo grabbed the game disc and put it into the console. Tommy picked up the controller and began searching, for Zane Crosby's team.

"Your brother's, a football player?" Bex asked.

Matt, turned to her. "*Ex* football player. He got—"

"It was terrible!" Tommy interrupted. "Zane was a Heisman Trophy winner, graduated top of his class. At the combines, he did the forty, in 4.5 seconds. So much talent, so much promise. But, on the first play of the season opener. On his first day as a professional football player, Zane catches the ball, for a punt return, to start the game. He runs what, fifteen, twenty yards? Ziggin' and zaggin' then… bam!"

Tommy clapped his hands, loudly for effect, startling Bex and Facundo. "He gets hit by one guy, totally knocking him off his feet, then smack! Another guy hits him in mid-air. I've never seen anybody, spin in the air four times, and get drilled into the ground like that. Brutal, compound fracture to his right tibia and fibula. God, I couldn't stand to watch, but I couldn't look away either, you know."

"Thank you Tommy, for the play, by play." Said Matt.

"How's your brother now? Can he still play?" Bex asked, concerned.

"He's recovered, but the Doctors say, he won't be the same. He probably won't play again." Matt said distantly.

Facundo said something incoherent.

"Thanks Facundo, I'm sure he'd appreciate that."

Tommy put on the game and selected Zane Crosby's team, The Carolina Panthers.

"You were a hot prospect too, Matt. I remember reading about you in college. You could've gone pro." Said Jason.

"Yeah... it wasn't for me. It was always more my father's dream, for us to go the NFL, than Zane's or mine. He was the winning-est football coach, in my High School's history. He coached my brother and I since we were little. When Zane got hurt, I think it broke his heart, more than it did Zane's. My dad pushed him to go back, but when Zane couldn't play anymore. He started looking to me, to carry the mantle. I couldn't take the pressure of living up to his expectations, too much stress. That's why I moved to New York, the first chance I got."

Jason ripped the bong. "Pussy."

Matt flipped him off, and took another bite of pizza.

"Wow, that's some story," said Bex. "So how does Claire, fit into all this?"

"Oh snap! There he is, number twenty-two!" Tommy said, pointing at Zane Crosby's football avatar.

"Claire was always just, *there*. We hooked up at party, she told me how she got into a dance school, in the city and that she was leaving, in a few days. So I was like, 'do you need a roommate?' And she was like, 'sure why not?' And that's how I ended up here, more or less"

"Just like that? Claire barely knew you and she invited you to come, with her?" Bex added.

"I may have told her, I loved her... At some point." Matt said reluctantly.

"At some point! Matt, you totally strung her along." Bex chided him.

"No it wasn't like that! We got along great, for a while, but then I started working at the gym, and shit just got crazy. I've never seen so many beautiful, fit, rich women. I lost, my God Damn mind. Then, I started hanging out with Jason, and that was it. Poppin' bottles at clubs, going down to Miami, and getting drunken mani-pedis."

Jason shook his head, urging Matt to stop, but Matt continued. "It made me realize, I wasn't ready to settle down."

Jason coughed up, the sip of beer he was trying to swallow. "I just want to say that I take no responsibility, for his behavior, that was totally all him."

"That's what I'm saying though, Jay. If it weren't for you, I'd be somebody I'm not. I'd be living a lie, continuing to do right by others, but not doing right by me." Matt smiled, at Jason, while he chugged, his beer. "You taught me to say fuck everybody else, and be happy."

"That was *so, not* my intention." Jason said flatly.

"Its cool man, it's for the best. I've never been happier." Matt said, patting Jason on the back.

"That's so sweet..." Bex said, sarcastically. "But what about the girl that took a chance, with a guy she barely knew. Who said, he loved her? Claire is the reason why you're here in the first place. She brought you, from who-knows-where Bumble Fuck County, to New York Fucking City, and now you're going around, acting single. I'm sorry you felt trapped, but you should've at least, been honest with her. It's called being a grown up."

"Ouch Bex, you're gonna tear him a new one, in his own house... at least wear lube." Jason joked. "This always happens, Bex gets drunk, and starts hurting feelings—as if she weren't brutally honest enough." Jason rolled his eyes. "And I thought spying for Vanessa, was bad shit."

Bex paused, looked at Jason, while she took a big drink.

"Alright here we go!" Said Tommy, preparing for kick-off, oblivious to the room.

The dramatic video game music, reverberated throughout the small apartment, drowning out, Bex's music. The announcer introduced the matchup: The Carolina Panthers versus the New York Jets.

"That *was* harsh, B." said Matt.

Bex shrugged, "Hey Jay, what did you mean, spying for Vanessa?"

"This is Geno's Jets! Remember, how that team, *sucked*!" Said Jason.

"Fitzy is in, the next edition," said Tommy, click-clacking on the controller.

"You know, despite how bad that QB was, he didn't deserve to get punched in the mouth." Jason added.

Facundo mumbled.

"Not nice Facundo, I would never punch you in face. Even if you owed me money," Jason said.

Facundo looked back at Jason, then said something, in Spanish.

A look of shear, shock came over Jason's face. "Okay... well damn, remind me to never borrow money from you. What the fuck, does first week's double, second week's trouble, even mean?

"Oh, there he is! He must've been so excited, when this game came out." Said Tommy, pointing to Zane Crosby on the screen.

"Not really." Matt said

"What, why?" he asked.

"You'll see." Matt replied.

Bex got up, moved to the edge of the futon, next to Jason."

The New York, Jets Kicker was set to punt. Tommy pressed the green button, to start. The virtual player, took a few steps, wound up his right leg, and kicked the ball.

The fans roared as the football ascended, high and far. It crossed the thirty-yard line, the forty; the fifty-yard line. But, due to the virtual, swirling winds, it began to drift left. Hurdling, back down towards earth. The game's camera angle, flipped to Zane Crosby's perspective. The virtual kickoff returner, shuffled toward the direction of the ball, catching it on the five-yard line. Tommy's fingers began to tap the buttons, and swirl the thumb sticks. Making the player sprint, to avoid the onslaught of approaching defenders. He reached the twelve, the thirteenth yard line. Juking left, dodging one player. He found himself on the fifteen, the sixteenth yard line, running behind a teammate, for protection. His teammate got violently, trucked aside. Zane spun right, bouncing off a defender, somehow managing to stay on his feet.

"Oh snap! Eighteen, nineteen!" Tommy shouted.

"Wait for it." Said Matt.

"Jason, what did you mean, spying for Vanessa?" Bex asked, again.

"You caught that, huh?" Said Jason.

Tommy turned right, juked left, then… POW! A defender from off screen plowed through Zane, flinging him into the air like a rag doll. Another off screen defender rammed into him in mid air spinning so him fast, so violently, that when his body hit the turf, he crumpled like a tin can, shattering his virtual, Tibia.

A collective gasp is heard from the virtual fans, sports announcers, and everyone in Matt's place. Zane grabbed his leg, writhing in virtual pain, holding the mangled limb in the air.

The virtual announcer's voice rang out, through the room: "Let's hope, he makes a speedy recovery, Steve. He's definitely, a talented young man, and it would be tragic, if he didn't make it back."

A second voice replied. "I don't think so, Tom. That is what you call, a schedule one, career ending injury."

Matt winced.

Jason took another sip of his beer, "That's kind of the reason, why I was hoping, we could hang out tonight."

"You mean it wasn't to laugh, at your absolute humiliation; and mock the way you were caught playing with yourself?" She said.

Jason was mortified. "You said you would take that part, to the grave Facundo! … The grave!"

Facundo mumbled, faintly. "Que grave? Es divertidísimo, pues…"

"So, that's it?" Tommy said. "He's out of the entire game!"

"Yup, it happens every time." Said Matt, flatly.

Tommy threw down the controller. "That sucks!"

Jason stood up. "All right everybody, gather 'round, take a knee."

Matt instinctively, got down on one knee, like he used to, when he played football. Everyone else was already seated.

Jason continued. "I have a confession to make—"

"You're quitting!" cried Tommy.

Jason shook his head.

"You're being deported?" said Matt.

Facundo mumbled.

"Again! I'm not doing gay porn." Jason exclaimed.

Bex sat there listening, waiting for Jason's announcement.

"I got a promotion."

Matt held up, his beer. "Congrats man! It's about time. You've only been working there, what ten years?"

Tommy shook Jason's hand. "Never in a million years, did I think, it would ever happen man... Happy for you, bro."

"Thanks, I guess..." Said Jason.

Facundo just shook his head, and rolled his eyes at the back-handed compliments.

Bex stared at Jason, waiting attentively.

Jason sighed. "It's not something, I asked for. Vanessa promoted me, to get us in line." He paused for a moment, dreading having to explain. " And to use my powers of good, for evil."

"Come on Jay, what is it really?" Bex insisted.

"I'm supposed find and report, whoever is selling steroids, at the gym. So, Vanessa can press charges, to make an example of them."

"She wants you to snitch?" Said Matt. "I wouldn't put it, past her."

"Someone is selling steroids, at the gym?" Bex asked. "That shit, is so fucking dangerous."

"And stupid!" Tommy agreed.

Jason looked at him, reading his transparent behavior. "Yeah, and if I don't find who it is. A story in the paper, is gonna come out. Creating another big scandal. Investors, will jump ship, our stock will drop. Making it easy, for Fit Corp to come in, and takeover. And you can bet, they'll be getting rid, of all of us."

Everyone was silent, for a few seconds. They were too high, to process the news, without really concentrating. Facundo pointed to himself, saying something in Spanish.

Jason put his hand, on Facundo's shoulder, as reassurance, "No Facundo, you'll never be fired. No god fearing American, would ever want to take your job."

Facundo smiled and pumped his fist. But then realized, everyone was still processing, what Jason had said, and returned to being serious. Matt stood up, walked back to the kitchenette, opened the cabinet, and pulled out a duffle bag.

"Look, I don't even know if she's telling me the truth, or if she's fucking with me." Jason said, shaking his head.

"To what end, Jay?" asked Bex, "Why does she fuck with you, so much? It's like you scorned her, and she's making you suffer."

Jason sighed, as he sat back down. "Yeah. I know exactly why. And I deserve it."

"What? Come on Jay!" Said Bex. "What happened? It couldn't have been that bad."

Tommy patted, Jason on the back. "Yeah man, don't beat yourself up."

Facundo nodded his head, in agreement.

"No, it's true" Jason replied. "I'm a fraud, a faker, a mercurial fuckwad that destroys everyone, I get involved with."

Facundo nodded his head, in agreement.

"Vanessa recognizes it, and exploits it. She knows, the only thing, I got going for myself, is this gym. So she manipulates me, just like she does, every other *asshole*. In order, to get what she wants. Sometimes… quite literally." Jason shuddered, looking off into space. "I'm going to tell, Vanessa the truth. I can't do this. I can't be her stooge. She'll probably fire me, but maybe she's right. I've been here long enough, maybe it is time to go."

"Jay you're a real good guy, you have to know that." Tommy said.

"Maybe that's what, I want you to believe. Maybe that's just another, one of my fundamentally flawed, character traits. You know, making people believe, I'm this awesome guy. But, I'm really just this asshole, that uses people, to lift him self up. Then, discard them, after getting what I want."

"Is that true Jay?" said Bex, her eyes, starting to water.

Jason lowered his head, in shame. "Afraid so."

Matt walked back over, from the kitchenette. "Before you say, anymore dumb shit. Take a look at this."

Matt threw the duffle bag, on Jason's lap.

"What is it?" Jason asked.

"Steroids." Matt replied.

Stunned, Jason opened the bag, uncovering dozens, of pill bottles.

"Holy shit, Matt!" He said, picking up a bottle. "You've been selling—wait… these, are vitamin C tablets."

"Yep." Matt concurred.

"You've been selling, vitamins to clients?" Jason asked.

"That's kind of the reason, why I was hoping, we could hang out." Said Matt, getting everyone's attention. "Have you ever wondered, how you could make more money, while still doing, what you love? … I did."

Everyone looked at each other, wondering what exactly, was going on.

Matt cleared his throat, taking moment to gather his thoughts, before starting his pitch.

"Are you tired of living, paycheck to paycheck? I am. Tired, of always having to hustle, for business, and not going anywhere? I used to be, until I became a Biovit distributor. Biovit products are pharmaceutical-grade, vitamins made from organic compounds. For example, our Gelotein Pro is a protein supplement, made from grass-fed horse marrow."

Bex barely kept her composure, trying not to gag, at the thought of horse protein.

Matt handed each of them, a bottle of Gelotein Pro.

"Two capsules contain, eight grams, of high quality protein."

Out of nowhere, a dazed Tommy, caught a moment of sobriety, and looked around. "What a minute, is this a fucking, sales pitch?"

"No, its not." Matt explained. "I'm simply, sharing information about an opportunity. That I feel, will benefit all of you, in the long term."

Jason stood up, grabbed Matt by the shoulders. "So, you're *not* selling steroids?"

Matt shook his head. "No, I'm not."

"Oh thank you Jesus!" said Jason, relieved. "Do you know what this means? It means, there's no steroids, no steroids, no scandal, no scandal, no story, no story, no corporate takeover."

Jason dropped to his knees. "Yes! I did it. I saved the gym!" He cried, joyfully. Everyone shakes their head's, watching him, as he carried on the celebration.

"Wait, this is a sales pitch!" Said Tommy. "Damn it, somehow I always get roped, into these network marketing schemes. What's the compensation plan like?

"Well there's actually, six income earning possibilities that..." Matt continued.

Bex leaned over to Jason. "You okay there, cowboy?"

Jason smiled wide, "I've never been better."

"So, what are you going to do?" She asked.

"First, I'm going to straighten this whole shit out with Vanessa once and for all. Then there's a little matter, by the name of Mandy that I need to attend to." He said.

"Jay... don't you dare, do anything to that girl." She said.

"Don't worry B. There's nothing I'm going to do that any other decent human being hell bent on revenge, wouldn't do." He said, with a wink. "Trust me."

"Jay!"

"Um guys, I'm in the middle of my presentation here." Matt interrupted.

"Oh well, look at the time. " Said Bex, checking her phone. "I gotta go, it's getting late."

"Okay well, maybe next time. Here are some brochures, you can take with you, in the meantime." Matt said, disappointed that Bex, was leaving, "Please, don't throw those away, I only have a few left."

Bex shut down the music, and packed up her DJ equipment.

"That's kind of the reason, why I was hoping we could hang out tonight." Tommy said to himself, watching Bex pack up her things

"Have a goodnight, see you tomorrow." She said, going around, hugging and kissing everyone, before she left.

After Bex closed the door behind her, Matt made another attempt, at the presentation, "Okay as I was saying, Biovit is an extraordinary—"

"Sorry there ol' chap, I gotta go too, I need to plan. It's my move." Jason interrupted, heading for the door.

"Okay well here, take some—"

"No time, gotta go!" Jason said, giving Matt, Tommy, and Facundo fist bumps.

Leaning back on the futon, with his arms crossed, was Tommy. He stared at Matt, unsure of his intentions. While, Facundo sat there, scrolling through his phone, with one hand, eating a chicken wing, with the other.

"Okay so… as I was saying." Matt continued.

Facundo stood up, before Matt could continue, with his presentation; Laughing at a silly meme, on his phone. He walked over to the kitchenette, grabbed another plate; Piled on, five more chicken wings, two slices of pizza, and grabbed a six-pack of beer. He then, turned, walked out of the apartment, without as much as a goodbye, adiòs, or hasta mañana. He didn't even look up, from his phone.

Matt stood there baffled, as he watched Facundo leave without saying a word. He then looked back at Tommy, who just sat there quietly, staring back. "Go on…" said Tommy, "… I'm listening."

20

Another Fine Mess

The next day, Jason went into Vanessa's office to explain what had happened,--at least part of what had happened, because, despite what Vanessa said about firing him, if he didn't find the culprit, there was no way he was going to turn Matt in.

He told her about the vitamins, and that there were never any steroids. She examined a bottle of the Biovit Gelotein-Pro for herself.

"Are you sure, this is what's been going around?" She asked.

Jason replied, confidently. "I'm positive, whoever's been selling these at the gym, was mistaken for a 'roids dealer."

"How do you know, for sure?"

He scoffed. "You asked me to get to the bottom of this and I did. There is nothing left to tell you. Whoever it was knows we're on to him and won't do it again. Besides, what is the penalty for selling vitamins here anyway? Come on Vanessa, are we done here? "

"I'm sorry, but I think I may have given you the wrong impression. Because as long as you work here, you will do, as you're told. Or I can write you up for insubordination. So no, we are *not* done here." She reclaimed.

Jason shook his head in disgust, "Now you're just fucking with me. "

"You really do think too highly of yourself, don't you? Always thinking everybody's jealous of you. '*Oh look at me, I'm the cool guy that's keeps getting fucked over, by jealous people.*'" Vanessa mocked him.

"What are you talking about?"

"It's true, you men are all the same. Just a bunch o' bru'ish fuks…"

Jason rolled his eyes. "Here we go… Is this were you tell me I'm an immature asshole, that I should grow up and appreciate everything you do for us? Because if it is, let me stop you, right there. I realize I'm an asshole: a big, fat, hairy, sloppy, asshole. But, despite all that, it doesn't mean I can't be a good person too. In fact, now that I know what I am, I can totally redirect *how* I asshole. "

Vanessa scoffed. "All this talk about, bloody assholes?"

Jason cleared his throat. "You see Vanessa, I don't have to put up with your shit. Especially if I'm doing what is expected of me; and from what I can see, everybody's personal training numbers are up so far this month—you're welcome, by the way. So the next time you think about harassing me, my friends, *your* employees, I will speak up and say something. And if that makes me the asshole, so be it. Cause, I don't give a *fuck*..."

Vanessa glared at Jason with utter disdain. She got up from her desk without saying a word.

Jason watched her walk across the office, flinching involuntarily as she passed him on her way to the door. She locked it.

"You know I was wondering when you were going to grow balls big enough to stand up for yourself." Vanessa said, in a flirty, kittenish tone.

"Can I just add," Jason said, "that you're threatening the livelihood, of my friends... Forcing me to stay quiet."

"You mean work acquaintances." Vanessa quipped.

"Them too." He shot back.

"So, then there is really nothing left to talk about... except for one thing." Vanessa said, sauntering, seductively, toward Jason, "Tell me, where you got the bottle."

Confused by what was happening, Jason replied, "I don't know."

"Liar!" Vanessa exclaimed.

He scoffed. "I'm not lying!"

Vanessa grabbed him by the shirt. "You know who it is. Tell me!"

"Now you're putting hands on me, really? You're too much Vanessa, I'm leaving."

"You're not bloody leaving until you tell me."

"I am telling you. All I know is that this is what you've been after. My sources told me it was found in a locker room... in a garbage bag." Jason pulled Vanessa's hands off of him. "I'm done being your stooge."

"Are you now..."

"Yeah Vanessa, I am..."

Vanessa interjected by kissing Jason passionately on the lips. He pulled away, surprised by the turn in behavior.

"Fuck off Vanessa, I'm done with you."

Rejected by Jason yet again. Vanessa lashed out and slapped him in the face. Dazing him for a split second. Angrily, he turned back and grabbed her by her throat. Jason had finally snapped. The years of contempt and resentment had come to a head. She looked deep into his rage-filled eyes, stunned by his reaction.

"Is this the only way I can get through to you?" Jason said, trembling with anger.

Vanessa gasped for air, her face turned beet-red, but surprisingly, she didn't struggle. Instead, she stood there, stoic as always, without a hint of fear. She submitted. Sensing her surrender, Jason shoved her onto her desk, spreading her thighs wide open. She immediately pulled him closer, impatiently untying, and pulling down his sweat pants. Jason drove his tongue hard into her mouth. She hurriedly pulled out his engorging penis, trying to place it into herself. Jason brusquely thrusted his hips, hard and deep, without any regard for his, or her, enjoyment. Vanessa groaned from the friction of his abrupt insertion.

"Is this what you want, you twisted bitch!?"

Jason kicked into reverse and pushed back into her. This time, she was ready for him. She tilted her pelvis, wrapped her legs around him tightly, and grabbed his buttocks. Making sure she got all of him.

"Harder, fuck me harder!" She moaned.

Jason huffed as he hastily penetrated her. Pulling her hair, whipping her head back. She wriggled around on the desk. This was not lovemaking, by any means. No, this was more like contemptuous fucking, at its very best.

Jason could feel her warm, wet, vagina contracting, every time his dick hit her, like a jackhammer, again and again.

She winced and yelped softly, when his penis, hit her cervix. Jason knew this was uncomfortable for her, but instead of easing up, it only made him want to hit it harder.

The hate-fueled session lasted for 5 minutes before Vanessa tensed up and trembled from an orgasm. Seconds later, Jason pulled out, grinded his hips into hers, and finished on Vanessa's stomach.

He stood there, hunched over, catching his breath, as the spasms dissipated. While, Vanessa lay back on her desk. She stared at the ceiling as the pain of regret set in. *What the hell got into me?*

She glistened, as she basked in the after glow, cut short by the realization of what had just happened. Jason however, had already pulled up his pants, and was fully aware of the situation, distraught by what he had just done.

Neither of them could come up with a word, a reason, an apology, something that could explain how two reasonably sane people became possessed by their animalistic desires. The silence was deafening. Vanessa could only watch Jason as he picked up his things, trying to get himself ready to leave.

Jason, on the other hand, was so ashamed, so embarrassed that he had lost control. He couldn't even look at her while he unlocked the door. He left her on the desk, without saying a word.

Outside of her office, he paused for a moment, replaying the prior events in his head.

"Oh, hi Jay." Said Jennifer, "I really feel sore, from the workout, the other day. Is Vanessa in?"

All Jason could do, to keep from screaming, at the top of his lungs. Was feign a smile, and nod his head yes, before he continued, on his way. Jennifer watched him walk off, while knocking on Vanessa's door. *I wonder what's up, with him.*

21

You Don't Look So Good

"Namaste everyone, I'll see you on Thursday. Mildred, amazing job today, your tree pose has really improved. Oh and don't forget to rehydrate. Today was a hot one! Oh! And I'm also teaching JP's Saturday morning class, so tell your friends, okay bye... bye."

Mandy's students put away their mats, blocks, and blankets, chatting to each other about random things like "What's for lunch?" or "See you at the salon, later."

They waved goodbye to Mandy, as they patted themselves down with towels. Mandy waved back, turned around, and walked over to the thermostat to lower the temperature.

"Looks like you had a full house." Said Jason from a dimly lit corner of the room, as if appearing out of thin air.

Mandy gasped. "Oh my god, you scared me! How long have you been standing there?"

"Not long... or maybe the whole class." He said, sweating profusely. "How are you?"

"I'm good." She said, catching her breath.

"Good I'm glad, I'm glad. I'm good too, considering..."

"Good, what's up?"

"Oh nothing... just wanted to say hey, haven't seen you in a few days. And oh, what the fuck, about the other day."

"What do you mean, what other day?"

"You know usually I get a good vibe on people, but I gotta admit, I had you pegged all wrong. My fault for assuming, I guess." He said, walking past her.

Mandy stood there confused by Jason's aloof behavior.

"And now we're being coy! Wow you're just gonna let me hang out there, twisting in the wind, aren't you." He said, exasperated.

"Okay... what are you talking about?" Mandy asked.

"Come on now, did you really have to take it that far. The Fire Department! Oh that was rich. But you got me, you got me good too, happy now?"

"Fire Department... I don't know what you're talking about, but you're being rude."

Jason laughed, "Rude! And what you did isn't considered rude?"

Mandy thought hard, but still nothing came to mind.

"You're actually going to make me spell it out, aren't you?" He said, getting annoyed.

"I told you about JP in the park, that's all I know."

"Okay fine, I'll play along." Jason said under his breath, "The text Mandy, I'm talking about the text from the other day."

"What text?" Mandy wondered aloud.

"The text... the sext." He said, clearing his throat.

Mandy looked back at Jason with a blank stare. "When?"

"Two days ago!"

"Two days ago? I forgot my phone at home two days ago. I didn't have it with me all day."

Jason paused, "You didn't see a text from me then?"

Mandy shook her head. "No..."

"So you didn't call the Fire Department?"

"No! The only thing I know about the Fire Department is that Sheila from reception mentioned there was an emergency. And that firemen came in to check out a short circuit in the electrical room."

All of the sudden, the heat and humidity in the room began to aversely affect Jason. *Short circuit indeed...*

"So that whole... meet me for some... you know.. on the third floor.. it wasn't you?" Asked Jason, trying hard not to sound crude.

"For some what now?" She asked, in return.

"Oh my God! It wasn't you!"

"Okay, now you're making me feel paranoid." Mandy said, raising her eyebrows.

Jason scratched his head as he paced back and forth, becoming more and more visibly agitated.

"What's wrong?" Mandy asked.

Jason paused, for a moment. "Oh you're good. You really got me going here." He said, now praying to God that she did send those firemen.

"Jason, I'm not fucking with you, what text are you referring to?"

Jason felt his heart rapidly palpating in his chest. He grabbed a towel to wipe the accumulating sweat from his brow. *Fuck, shit, fuck! What do I say?*

"The text... it's nothing, I am fucking with you. In fact, let's forget it." he gulped. "Is it getting hotter in here?"

"It's hot yoga, of course it's hot in here. Why do you look so pale, all of the sudden?" Mandy asked.

A queasy feeling in Jason's stomach began to simmer. "Uh, I've been fasting. My body... Just needs something to eat."

"You're lying..."

"I am not lying!" He said, pretending to be genuinely offended. "Oh my god, it's so hot in here! "

Mandy paused. *Really?*

His breathing became heavy and sporadic. The bitter taste of bile began to show on his face.

"Are you okay? You don't look so good." Asked Mandy, concerned about his appearance.

Jason gulped, "I'm fine. I just really need to..."

Jason's eyes rolled into the back of his head. He fell like to the ground, out like a lamp.

Mandy gasped, "Jason wake up, wake up, Jason..." She said, slapping his face, and checking his breathing.

Jason gasped and shot up to a seated position.

"Oh shit! What happened?" He yelled out, startling Mandy.

"You were unconscious."

"Really?" He said, coming to his senses, "I'm so, so sorry, but I have to go. I'll talk to you later." He stood up.

"You should go to the emergency room."

"Good idea, I'll go right now." Jason agreed, hastily.

"Good, but just realize... this conversation, is not over." Mandy shouted, as Jason rushed toward the exit.

Jason ran out of the gym, with his arms around his stomach. He looked up and down the street, trying to figure out which direction he should take. *The park.*

22

Questions

As Jason ran up the street, trying to get away from Mandy for long enough to figure things out, an unmarked police car pulled up to the Grand. Two plain clothes officers stepped out of the vehicle and walked in. They asked the receptionist if they could speak with the general manager. Sheila immediately called Vanessa's office. Moments later, Jennifer arrived to escort the two officers. She led them up to the 5th floor, where Vanessa greeted them.

She shook their hands as they walked into her office and asked them to sit. "Good afternoon officers. I hope you didn't have to wait long."

"No trouble at all, Ms. Todd. I'm officer James Aiello, this my partner Ted Bronsky." Said one of the policemen.

"Nice to meet you both." Smiled Vanessa, "How can I help you today?"

"First off, I just want to say this is a pretty swanky gym. How much is it to join here?" Ask Officer Aiello.

"Well that depends on the type membership, but we usually give discounts to New York's Finest. I can set you up with an appointment right now, if you like." She said, picking up the phone.

"I don't know why he's even asking, it's not like he remembers how to workout anyway." Chuckled Officer Bronsky, pointing to his partners protruding belly.

"Easy..." said officer Aiello, "I'll meet you in the ring, any day of the week."

Vanessa tried not to roll her eyes. "Officers..."

"Sorry Ms. Todd, let's get to it." Said Officer Aiello. "We have a reliable source that has led us to suspect this gym as a major hub for steroids and other *illegal* performance enhancing drugs.

Vanessa scoffed nervously. "I assure you, gentlemen, that this is a libelous and baseless rumor, started by our competitors in order to disrupt our investor relations and stock price." She explained.

She continued to tell them all about what Jason had said to her.

"That's a pretty funny coincidence. Does anyone know who the perpetrator of the supplements is?"

"I personally don't know who it was, however, I know the person that does. I would gladly bring him in, if you like." Said Vanessa, too eager to help.

"That won't be necessary. No law was broken—if what you say is true. We'll just keep that in mind. For future reference." Said the Officer.

She went on to tell them, that it was all taken care of and that no investigation was warranted. After about twenty minutes of questioning, the officers seemed quite satisfied with Vanessa's explanation, even sharing a chuckle or two about how ridiculous it all seemed. Both Officers stood up and thanked Vanessa for her time and cooperation.

"Hey, I know we said we're done here, but the chief is going to be up our asses if we don't follow through on yet another tip," said Officer Bronsky, as they walked toward the door.

"Are you gonna write the report?" Aiello asked.

"You can be a real cocksucker sometimes." Bronsky whispered.

"Hey, Ms. Todd do you mind if we take a quick look around the place? It's protocol, you understand?" The Officer asked.

"Of course, it's quite a big place though, let me have my assistant show you around." Vanessa suggested.

"That won't be necessary Ms. Todd. Officer Aiello and I got it covered. Besides, my partner could use the cardio." He said, nodding toward Officer Aiello.

"Very well then, if you insist." She agreed.

23

Worst Week Ever, Be Like

While Vanessa dealt with the police, Jason was at a playground a few blocks away. He stood over a garbage can, dry heaving intensely, trying to make himself vomit. He stopped for a moment to catch his breath, hoping the urge to hurl had passed. His mind reeled, completely preoccupied with Mandy and the fiasco he had gotten himself into. He tried to figure it out: if it wasn't Mandy, then who sent those text messages? It had to be Steven, her fiancé. Who else could've had access to her phone? But why hasn't he confronted her about it? There was no way to explain it without totally embarrassing Mandy.

He sat on a park bench. A bead of sweat dripped from his right brow. His mind processed everything, flashing back to when he texted Mandy. Flashing forward to when the Firemen broke into the room. He thought of the vitriolic hate sex with Vanessa, which made him feel even worse. *I fucked up with Mandy*. He thought to himself, shaking his head.

The urge to puke hadn't completely subsided. Suddenly, a group of children from a nearby daycare pitter-pattered by with their caregivers close behind. They herded the toddlers toward a little playhouse near a cigarette butt-laden sandbox. Jason couldn't help but watch these little humans maneuvering through the world. *Fascinating*.

Then, for a moment, Jason's noisy, dysfunctional brain went blank, briefly, forgetting the shit storm he'd brought on himself. A warm, relaxing, sensation began to ease the tension in his jaw. He took a deep breath and sighed. *Damn, I could a use joint*.

He began to wonder what was it going to be like having his own kid. What type of father would he be? Would he be a great father? Or would he be like his own father, Miguel, a young, brash hothead, who thought he knew everything but was really too young, too ignorant about life, to know anything. It was that self-doubt. A voice in the back of his head that gnawed at him. *Who are you kidding? You, a father! Look at yourself; you're a fucking disaster. You shouldn't be allowed to be a father... I shouldn't be allowed to be a father.*

Jason watched the children play, envying their innocence, their carefree bliss, and worriless lives. One of the children, a little girl with pigtails, carried a doll. She pretended to feed it a toy baby bottle. When she was done, the little girl placed the doll over her shoulder and pretended to burp it. *Aw... so adorable.*

After the kid finished burping the doll, she placed it face down on her forearm and began petting it like a cat, or some other small animal. The same odd way Venetta the nanny had done with Teresa's newborn. *Okay, am I the only one that thinks that's fucking strange?*

Jason jumped to his feet, swung toward the garbage can, and spewed an extraordinary amount of vomit. The force with which Jason threw up caused his vomit to overshoot the garbage can, missing it completely. The sound of Jason's deep billowing and vomit splashing on the ground startled everyone in the park. Even the children took pause. His mouth contorted and his body convulsed as he held the waste receptacle with all his might, puking his guts out.

But after what seemed like an eternity of heaving, Jason hovered over the receptacle, spitting out any chunks left in his mouth, until the urge to hurl had once again dissipated. He wiped his chin, sat back down to catch his breath, and stared at the ground, hoping he hadn't made too much of a scene. *Well at least my stomach's empty, calorie deficit, check.*

Just then, Jason noticed two pairs of legs coming into his peripheral vision.

"You alright there, buddy?" Said a uniformed police officer.

"Yeah why, just here to enjoy the view." Said Jason, pretending to act casual, but not too casual.

The two officers looked over at the children, at each other, then back at Jason.

"One of these your kids?" asked the other officer.

"Uh, no… is there a problem with me sitting here, officers?"

"Not if you have a child, playing in the park." The officer replied.

"Oh… *Ohhh*, but I'm not… you guys think… I see." He stammered.

"Can we see some ID?"

Jason patted his pockets, "ID! I left it at work, I can go and get it."

"No ID!" Said the officer, as they follow Jason out of the park. "We're gonna pat you down, is that okay?"

Jason began to feel uneasy, "Not really, I'm an American citizen. Besides my ID is at work!"

"What's your name?" Asked one of the policemen.

"Jason Garcia…"

The cop pulled out his radio, "Hey dispatch, we have an amigo here, about five foot, six inches. Goes by the name of Jason Garcia…"

Jason watched the police officer on the walkie-talkie.

"Do you have any sharp objects or anything else I should be aware of before I stick my hands in your pocket?" Asked his partner.

"No…" Jason replied, preoccupied with the officer on the radio. "I told you my ID's at work, right down the street. I thought stop and frisk was over."

The policeman scoffed. "You were found loitering in a playground without any children of your own. And you're not carrying any identification…"

"I wasn't loitering!"

The policeman on the radio came back, "Dispatch wants us to bring him in. His name was crossed referenced with the federal database. The name Jason L. Garcia appears as a person of interest. In a murder investigation, down in Texas."

"What! That's not me." Jason insisted, "There have to be a million Jason Garcias."

"Okay, we believe you. But, we still have to take you in for questioning."

Jason scoffed, as the policeman handcuffed him, "Unbelievable! Just take me to my job, I can show you, I'm a citizen."

People walking by slowed down to get a glimpse of all the commotion.

One of the officers took Jason by the arm, "Alright buddy, watch your step."

Jason knew better than to resist, he didn't want to give them any excuse to press some bullshit charges. *I can't believe the week I'm having.*

Meanwhile, back at the Grand, Officers Aiello and Bronsky were entering the men's locker rooms. They asked Facundo to take them to a specific locker. Hesitant at first, Facundo called up to Vanessa's office to get the okay. He led the officers down to the locker in question. Using a master key, Facundo opened the locker door and stepped aside. One of the officers pulled out a small, navy blue duffle bag, unzipped it, and pulled out a handful of bottles containing human growth hormones, vials of bovine testosterone, and several syringes.

Bronsky turned to Aiello. "Jackpot much?"

24

Greenmailin' Like a Boss

The captain came on over the intercom. "Attention ladies and gentlemen, we hope you've been enjoying the flight. We will be commencing our descent shortly, arriving at Cape Town International Airport in approximately thirty minutes. Please make your way back to your seats, buckle your seat belts, and put up your seats and tray tables. All electronic items must be turned off and any bags put back underneath the seat. Thank you very much for flying Alpha Air."

J.P. brought up his seat and put up his tray table. He reached for his phone to shut it off, but before he could, He saw a text notification from NY Post.

'Roids All The Rage at Mega Gym.

J.P. sat up and began to read the article.

"Excuse me sir, but we need you to put away your cell phone, airline policy." Said a flight attendant walking by.

"Yes of course, right away!" He said, without looking up from his phone.

As he continued to read the article, a crooked smile formed on his face.

On the morning of November fourteenth, police received a call from an anonymous source. The tip led them to a locker inside The Grand Metropolitan Health and Fitness facility in Soho, where, yesterday afternoon, they conducted a routine investigation, to follow up on the tip.

Authorities seized one gym bag filled with illegal, performance-enhancing drugs and syringes, worth approximately thirteen thousand dollars on the street.

Investigators believe that the drugs in question were intended to be re-distributed to buyers within the gym. Police continue to interview em-

ployees and members of the gym whom they believe may have had access to the locker rooms in recent days. No suspects, however, have been taken in for questioning as of press time.

J.P. sat back in his seat, barely controlling his sniggering, as he continued reading.

The passenger sitting next to him glared as he continued to scroll down on his phone. "Excuse me, the stewardess asked you to put away your phone."

"Mind yours rooineck." J.P. said to the lady.

The passenger gasped at the derogatory term and sat back in her seat, silently.

"I don't see nothing..., I f*** ing clean, that's it!" Said Facundo Sanchez, the outspoken head of the housecleaning department at the Grand.

This is not the first time the Grand has been in the headlines. Three years ago, Fit Corp, the largest fitness conglomerate in the country, attempted to purchase the Grand in a hostile takeover. But the timely recovery of the economy lifted the Grand's stocks price at a key moment, putting it just out of reach of Fit Corp. However, with a scandal like this, it will be interesting to see whether any volatility in the stock price occurs, which could possibly put the company back in the crosshairs of Fit Corp.

"That's preposterous," said Vanessa Todd, General Manager of the Grand. "The Grand is an institution in this city. It has always been, and it will always belong to its members. This is nothing more than old-fashioned corporate sabotage."

Sources close to the Post report that if Fit Corp manages to buy the Grand's outstanding shares, it could legally threaten a takeover. The only way the Grand could refuse would be to buy back its shares at a much higher price, effectively dismantling the business from the inside out, a process known as Greenmailing.

Even though the Grand Metropolitan has made it through the worst economic recession since the Great Depression, it looks like only time will tell if the world's most luxurious gym will be able to survive this time around.

25

Epilogue

Sitting at her dining room table, Vanessa fumed after reading the story in the New York Post. She felt her blood boil as she put down her tablet and picked up her glass of Pinot. *How could this have happened, how could've I have been so bloody careless? That asshole tricked me, I know it! He had to have known all along. He wanted this to happen. Maybe he's the dealer! No… Now I'm giving him way too much credit. Why the hell did I have sex with him? Ugh!*

Preoccupied with the deluge of problems coming her way, Vanessa wandered over to the living room. The uncertainty of the Grand and the threat of getting high-jacked by some greedy, money grubbing conglomerate churned her stomach. Everything she had worked for, all the time, money, and bullshit, she had to put up with in order to get to her prominent position. Now it was all about to be snatched away in one fell swoop, all because of Jason and his complete and utter ineptitude. *I'm finished.*

The stress was gut wrenching, almost unbearable. Wine dribbled from her mouth as she finished her drink. A single purple streak ran down her chin, dripping onto her breast. She looked down, wiped the drip with her finger, and sucked it off.

"Another glass bartender!" She yelled.

The wine clearly wasn't doing its job, because the pain of her reality would not yield, even as she emptied her second bottle.

Vanessa began to make her way back to uncork a new bottle. She caught a glimpse of her reflection on a mirror on the far side of the living room. It hung on the wall above a small wooden table, decorated with a white Orchid, placed in a white porcelain vase. She paused for a moment and stared at herself intently. The heated energy of her pent up rage subsided, at least for a moment.

She turned her attention away from her mounting troubles to her reflection in the mirror. Her right hand gently pulled at her robe, sliding it off and exposing her left shoulder; the left hand did the same, uncovering her right shoulder.

The ruby red robe she'd been wearing fell softly to the floor, surrounding her, in a heap of silk. She stood in front of the mirror, wearing nothing but a black-laced bra with matching black-laced underwear, fitted perfectly on her tight, svelte body.

She beamed at what she saw, thoroughly inspecting every curve, taking in every contour of her body. appreciating the years of work she had put in at the gym. She turned to the right, then turned her torso back, facing the mirror, posing. She turned to the left, extended her leg, and flexed her left gluteus. *Coming along rather nicely, wouldn't you say?*

"Indeed…" Said a voice.

Startled, she immediately stopped. She looked around the living room. She turned toward the mirror. *Did that came from the mirror?*

Vanessa stood there, staring deeper into the reflection, squinting her eyes, as she stepped closer to the mirror. *What is that?*

She turned back to look at an empty chair, sitting next to a window, with the curtains down. *Nothing…*

She looked back into the same place in the mirror. She began to feel a rush of anxiety. A familiar feeling of dread came over her, bubbling out to the surface, from behind her strong façade. *Why is this happening now?*

She could feel the presence of another person, but there was no one there. Her senses were on high alert. *How odd…*

"Odd, am I?" Said the voice.

Vanessa realized she hadn't taken her anti-psychotic medication in over a day. With everything that had been happening around her, she forgot. And now her symptoms were reemerging. But this time, they were stronger, more vivid. She'd never had voices whisper in her head before. It had to be all the stress she was under.

Vanessa paced back and forth, trying to comprehend what was happening. But, before she could utter a complete thought, the voice interrupted. "Simple girl, simple girl!"

Vanessa looked back at the empty chair, as if waiting for someone to appear. "You think it's easy running a business? I'd like to see you try it." Vanessa said to the chair. "Am I hallucinating?"

"I thought we were a cunning bitch?" Said the voice.

"I, I still am…"

"Then how did a cunning bitch get out witted by a complete imbecile?"

Vanessa stammered, as she tried to explain, "I, I…"

"You let your guard down again, didn't you? You depended on someone, and they betrayed you… again!"

Vanessa fell to her knees, she knew she needed her medication, "Stop talking, I'm trying to explain!"

"Brutish beasts don't obey; they trample, upend, and destroy throughout their entire lives. You cannot reason with it, you cannot control it, and you definitely cannot love it… as you well know." Said the voice, in an accusatory tone. "No…There needs to be retribution."

"Retribution! What's the bloody point, we're all out! Game over! The club will be bought, sold, and everybody will go. Those who stay will make far less money, it doesn't get any worse."

"You've done far worse. I made sure of that."

Terrified by what was happening her Vanessa got up, ran to the dining area, and picked up a bottle of prescription medication.

"Off to numb yourself again, eh?" Said the voice.

Vanessa ignored the auditory hallucination, and opened the bottle.

"This shite is poisoning us. How much of this, can your liver take, you only get one, you know." The voice continued.

She poured three pills into her hand, then paused for a moment. She put one pill back, and opened her third bottle of wine.

"Eventually, those won't help anymore. Then you'll have to try something stronger, more addictive, more side effects; making yourself sick, just to keep me away!"

Vanessa squatted in a fetal position. Her eyes welled up with tears, mixing with her mascara. She tried to fight them back, but black tears streaked down her face anyway.

"Look at yourself, so pathetic. You have now officially become the thing you hate most… Weak!"

Vanessa covered her ears and shook her head, hoping the voice would stop.

"Don't worry, you've subdued us. We feel the poison, coursing through our veins. Numbing you, oppressing me, killing us."

Vanessa rocked back and forth, huddled tightly on the floor, trembling, like a scared child. "Go away, go away…"

"While you sit there, determined to kill us, I've been here, keeping us alive, no matter what. I was in London, when you O.D'd, I saved us. And now, I'm here in New York, about to save us again."

Vanessa begged, "Please just stop… just stop."

"Face it cunt! Without me, we'd be dead, floating down the Thames, with a needle sticking out of our arm. You're pathetic, weak, *nothing!*" Shrilled the voice.

Vanessa screamed at the top of her lungs, bounded to her feet, picked up the wine glass, and threw it at the mirror. "Get away from me!"

The glass hurled toward the mirror, shattering into small pieces, as it struck. Wine splashed across the mirror, cracking it. Leaving a distorted web like pattern, of fissures in the mirror. Vanessa's heart thudded against her chest as she stood there, exhausted and afraid. The voice stopped. There was nothing, only silence. Wine dripped, from the mirror, as Vanessa glared at her fractured image, desperately, hoping the voice in her head was gone. The white orchid on the table was stained with the crimson splatter of wine.

The mirror although damaged, for the most part, is nonetheless still a mirror. It continues, to reveal the world that surrounds it, nothing more, nothing less. Reflecting back, everything the light catches. The cracks are a representation of her imperfection. Undesirable by most standards, but despite it's own irregularities. The mirror never ceased, to expose the truth. A truth, Vanessa's can no longer deny. *I am broken.*

Because, no matter how beautiful, or how perfect things may seem on the surface. The superficial, can never be taken at face value. The truth, always prevails, no matter how deep, it's buried.

Take it from Vanessa, still visibly shaken, but undaunted. Gazing further into the mirror, until she's just inches away. She felt the fear leave her body. As she glanced between the cracks, that revealed more fragmented pieces, of her true self. The broken, chipped, and distorted images. Resembled her, broken, chipped, distorted soul. The fear is then replaced, by anger, an anger fueled, by what she considered a betrayal. Stabbed in the back, by Jason Garcia. *"There will be retribution!"*

The End

www.ingramcontent.com/pod-product-compliance
Lightning Source LLC
Chambersburg PA
CBHW020909180626
46816CB00007BA/2322